MW01171160

Goodbye,
Ross Wellington

Joseph Hess

Copyright © 2023 by Joseph Hess
All rights reserved.

No portion of this book may be reproduced in any form
or by any means without the written permission of the
author.

This is a work of fiction. Any similarities to actual
organizations, places, events, or to real persons, living or
dead, are purely coincidental.

Designed and Published by Joseph Hess

ISBN 9798393985578

To the patient ones

Goodbye,
Ross Wellington

Prologue

The place, as intended, had the atmosphere of a roadside bar. Neon lights against a midnight sky. Patrons sharing a drink, or drinking alone, while the world moved on around them. Except this place wasn't at the side of any road, and the starless sky was as artificial as the sign that read "Grudgeville Grille". It wasn't just a place for drinking, either, though its creator had embraced such usage along the way.

The portal, a stone's throw from the entrance, at the adjacent perimeter of the campus, that was the thing.

The outbuildings had all been added later, staging and storage for the goods being transported from one world to the next. The main building was located much closer to the portal, leaving large, open areas between it and many of the other structures. And it was there, in the softly lit conference room toward the rear of the first floor, that things had gotten heated tonight.

Actually, by then it was already morning, though only just, and things getting heated had become the new normal. The room was full, as it had been of late, council members seated at the long rectangular table at the center, and in the chairs around the perimeter, leaving several with room only to stand. Since hearing from one of Gurba's agents that he had been momentarily struck down, and that a second-wave attack was about to commence at the place called Richard's Motel, where Ch'gal had trailed Kennedy James and the girl, the Council had been waiting for further word.

They worried over what it could mean that Gurba's people had been wiped out in the blink of an eye, their reinforcements, watching from distance, unable to describe what had happened in any better terms than that. Much more importantly, they fought to encapsulate what they were now facing, it having become painfully obvious they had been manipulated. A fact which stung all the more because they had already suspected it.

They were still going, this one talking to that one while talking past the other to the one behind, when their leader, Kalar Doge, hung up the phone. He hadn't blessed them by putting the call on speaker, so they hadn't noticed what he was up to. Now, they saw him, and gradually the room quieted until they were all waiting in silence, noting the ominously swollen flesh at the base of his horn. It was almost 3:00 a.m.

"That was our contact in the state police."

He was staring blankly at the center of the table for he didn't know how long, when someone said, "And?" It was Fio, always at his right.

"The attendant at the gas station across the highway... Apparently, he likes to turn up his music when there are no customers. As a result, he missed the commencement of events at the motel, but claims that he heard gunfire, and saw a 'swirling green light' before the couple who had rented a room earlier in the evening went speeding off on their motorcycle. He then called the police, but when they examined the scene there was nothing, and no one, to corroborate his account. Obviously, Wellington cleaned up the mess."

Ross Wellington. The source of their misfortune, but, as the creator of the Grille, their benefactor as well. He had merely outlived his usefulness.

"We had every reason to be suspicious," Doge said. "Even while he was purporting to aid us, he could have had only one motive for drawing us into this. Now there is no doubt that he intends to move against us. And with the Generator in place, the hitman is his greatest asset."

Nervous glances were exchanged, but this was not news. They had been certain of this possibility for hours, if not days.

"But what about the rest of it, Kalar? Clearly, we understood even less than we feared." Now it was Ceyon, to his left, who spoke up. As his two closest peers, in both years and experience, it was he and Fio in the recent days who would reliably ask what they all were thinking. As if to illustrate the point, everyone down table, as well as those surrounding them in the shadows at the edge of the room, were facing them again, eagerly watching the exchange. "We were wrong about Ch'gal's use to him, if not also the apparent risk to the girl. If Wellington was merely planning to kill him, it is safe to assume she was in no danger at all."

"You are right, my friend. We are left with the same questions that have existed since all of this started. Yet it changes nothing of our position. With Gurba's forces all but wiped out, there is no better time than right now for Wellington to strike. It is a mystery he hasn't already."

Voices rose again throughout the room. While awaiting further information, they had already begun their preparations. If the hitman had truly dispatched all of their people, he had surely done Ch'gal in as well. And the mere fact that it had happened meant it was entirely by Wellington's design. They had found it hard to believe he had ever wished to help them, yet had had no choice but to take what they were given for fear of Ch'gal's return putting them at risk the same as he carelessly had the first time. At last, it seemed all too clear what Wellington was truly intending to use the hitman for, even while the rest of it, as Ceyon had so helplessly put it, remained an incoherent jumble of details and events that would likely never coalesce.

"Sir, if I may." Doge recognized immediately it was Qazaen, the only female member of the Council. Plenty were those who served the Grille in other capacities, but this was a closed meeting, and as a result he quickly spotted her in her usual seat, farther down, just short of Thule and his timid young protégé.

Her greenish complexion always reminded him of the toadlike Gurba, while the rest of her features—that is, those of her species—had a markedly feminine quality not unlike many Earth women. If not for the second set of arms attached at her elbows, unlike Thule's protégé, Halan, who had the extra shoulders to match, she could have passed for human with the right kind of makeup. And perhaps a hat to cover the bony ridges spread longitudinally over the top of her head.

When the room had quieted once again, he said, "Of course."

"Why now?" she said simply. "I have deferred to the more senior members of the Council thus far, but I can't help but ask. It would seem that Wellington has been content to sit on the sidelines, so to speak, from the time he left in pursuit of Ch'gal until now. Luring him back, let alone using the girl to do it, appears to have had no connection to his designs against us. Especially if his plan hinges on the hitman. So why now, when it would seem he could have used him at any time?"

"Another good question," Doge said, "and, I fear, just as unlikely to be answered. Even before confirming that the Generator was truly functional, we had long assumed it was the very reason we could still operate at all. And while he is apparently incapable of affecting the portals, or our usage of them, his lack of interference with our agents in the field could only be attributed to some desire to glean as much from them as he could, a continuous source of information. At the very least, it would seem that even he can't be everywhere at once. You ask, why now? It could be simply that whatever his preoccupation with Ch'gal and the girl, it was keeping him on Earth, or close to it. But with that business apparently concluded, as confounding as it is to us, the fact remains that Kennedy James was instrumental to him, and is undeniably at his disposal. All the more reason we must expect them to strike, and to strike quickly."

Now, his forehead feeling no less inflamed, but no more either, he met the gazes of everyone around the table, managing to maintain his calm. "We are doing everything we can, though it is not much. Our agents continue to pour in. Others stand firm outside the portals. Knowing that Wellington could very well land the hitman at our doorstep from any location he wishes, it would be foolish to concentrate solely on Earth. Still, the bulk of our forces must, and will, remain here. We had hoped to avoid it, but such a move has long been expected. At this point, the best we can hope for is to be ready."

Such evil has decorated my existence, I can scarcely hope to undo it. Yet the eons bear witness as I desperately try.

I do not know what He wants from me.

One

Ashlee stared in awe. "Wow, you didn't do it justice."

They had just arrived at the spot Kennedy had described, the farthest point of a large cul-de-sac, where three houses spaced far apart like all the rest—presumably because that was what the residents of this particular neighborhood had all signed up for—stood perpetually unmolested except for the regularly scheduled professionals involved one way or another in the properties' upkeep. Apparently, the point was to have them at his disposal at all times—including the two at either end, whose only function was to provide him an even larger buffer than any of the neighbors, both for their protection and his own piece of mind—should he ever have to resort to coming here.

Never mind that they were being hunted on top of it all. By his tone on the ride over, today was that unfortunate day.

"Why didn't you mention this sooner?" Ashlee said.

"With everything going on?" To Kennedy, it seemed she was forgetting they had only *just* been reunited, and under less than ideal circumstances, to say the least. After leaving Ross behind at Richard's Motel, they had timed their arrival for the following night, his bike successfully purring past the neighbors in secret because he'd had it in scooter mode, finding him thankful, as always, for the revolutionary—and strategically suppressed—technology that gave him the choice. But since this had all started, and even after driving through the early morning hours and then hunkering down all day, they'd had vastly more important things to talk about. And still it seemed they had barely scratched the surface.

"Sorry, it just didn't come up."

They were standing at the end of the driveway, dark except for the soft moonlight. The coach lights on either side of the garage, as well as those of the two adjacent properties, were off, but the views along the street on the way in had provided a sense of what it would otherwise look like.

"But even Ross didn't say anything. 'Go to the cul-de-sac, Kennedy. You will be safe at the cul-de-sac.' When he said we should 'return to the city' I thought he was expecting us to just find some hole somewhere. You mean we could've been staying here the whole time?"

"Was the storage that bad?"

Their previous hideout wasn't bad at all, and in fact when he said it she recalled having enjoyed their few brief days there more than any other time in her life. Had they not been discovered, and the place destroyed, it could have lasted indefinitely. "No. No, I just mean—"

"I know what you mean. I'm teasing. But bear in mind, if we had been here, then this would be the spot that was blown up, and we'd be off hiding in the storage now anyway."

She couldn't argue with that. "I'm still surprised you have them, though."

"Really? The position we're in? That's like saying it's weird that a guy who just shot someone in self-defense was carrying a gun."

"You know what I mean. What? One day you thought, 'Hm, I think I should buy three houses, just in case.'"

"Not exactly," Kennedy said, though now that she was pointing it out, he couldn't deny how it looked. "As much as it's not my first choice, this isn't the first time I've been here. You remember when I told you how I stayed in the city while the storage was going up?"

"Yeah."

"Well, I suppose I didn't actually mean *in* the city. But I didn't want to have a bunch of new people asking me questions I'd have to make up answers for, either, so another apartment was out of the question. These units were already built, and I had the cash... I would sneak in late, and sneak out when everything seemed quiet. Though with the big lots and the trees in between, it's almost impossible to see down here anyway. Unless you're watching from the road. Other than literally being underground, or so far out of town it wasn't worth it, this was the next best thing."

Ashlee considered how the storage was a half hour away already, and that having his friend Knuckles nearby was part of the motivation for putting it where he did in the first place. If he had needed somewhere to call home while construction was under way, not between here and there, for logical, tactical reasons, it seemed, and yet not too far in any other direction, then she had to agree. It was a prime choice.

"Then I guess I'm glad you hung on to them," she said. "Convenient."

"You might be less enthused once we're inside."

"Why's that?"

He turned to her. "No furniture."

Using the service door in back, Kennedy opened the garage and stowed the scooter out of sight, putting it in motorcycle mode while he was at it. Neither configuration was ideal for two, but the drive through the city from the remote diner where they had been lying low all day had left both their asses sore. When they left here, it could very well be because they were making a break for it. Might as well be on a larger seat.

Afterward, he led Ashlee into the house, where they found themselves standing in the opening from the kitchen, peering into the empty living room, blackout curtains covering the large window.

"I would say get settled, but we're in the door, so that's pretty much it. Why don't you order some food? It's about time I touched base with Knuckles." Kennedy patted his satchel, both of them having brought their things in from their respective saddlebags. His traditional burner was lying dormant inside, buried beneath all his work gear, including his mask and vest, and even his coat and hat. "He's probably called a hundred times trying to figure out what happened at the storage, or if we're even still alive. No doubt he's got Shields wondering by now, too." It was the first time he had mentioned Shields since it all happened, but he had told Ashlee enough that she would get it. Shields had been his broker almost as long as he had known Ross, vetting contracts for him so that Kennedy didn't have to wade through them all. The work he did for him was indispensable. But more than that, Shields was a friend.

"My phone is gone, remember?" Ashlee said.

That's right. She had told him that. He had advised her days ago not to use it, or even turn it on, and as a result she had quit carrying it with her. Apparently, it had been lying next to the little lamp by her cot when the storage went up. Now it was just a charred lump of metal and plastic, covered in soot. He kept forgetting it wasn't clean like his—no GPS and no data—besides. Even if she still had it, using it now would be no safer than it was before.

"Here, take the laptop," he said, fishing it out of his bag. He had actually never gone online with it, but had figured that until they heard from Ross, if they were going to stay on top of anything, it was the only option they had. "I'll bet at least one of the neighbors is too careless to lock their Wi-Fi." After entering the password, he handed it over and told her the street address.

"Okay," she said. "I hope they're alright."

"I told you, Knuckles is tough. And he knows what to do if anything comes up." He produced a wad of cash, and handed it to her. Then, he said, "Don't worry. I'll fill you in."

After retrieving his phone, Kennedy dropped his bag in the empty dining room and made for the nearby patio door.

Ashlee then dropped her own before moving into the open kitchen with the computer.

A half hour later, she was drip drying in the bathroom and brushing her hair when Kennedy called from halfway up the stairs, "Ashlee?"

"In here."

When he entered the doorway, he froze. "I sure am glad there aren't any towels."

"And I'm sure glad I have my own razor. How are they?"

"Good. He said it still reeks like burnt plastic and melted aluminum, even at their place, but they're fine. And no one's been around since the police and fire trucks left either." Kennedy had known even as he and Ashlee were speeding away that the sight, perfectly visible from the highway, was going to draw such attention. And despite being a mile away, as potential witnesses, there had been plenty of questions for Knuckles and Ruth as well. Knuckles had played it cool, while Ruth… Well, Ruth just being Ruth had ensured her interview ended quickly.

"That's good," Ashlee said. "I was hoping it was a good sign you were still on the phone." Working at the kitchen counter, it hadn't taken her long to discover that not one but three of the neighbors had failed to safeguard their Wi-Fi, though only one, in fact, had a reliably strong signal. Placing an order had taken somewhat longer since she was absolutely starving and absolutely everything looked good, but when she was done, Kennedy was still talking. And he had appeared reassuringly calm.

Kennedy said, "It is, but I told him they should still keep an eye out. They *were* my closest neighbors. If the Grille gets it in their heads that *somebody* must know *something*, they might pay them a visit."

"I'd feel better if they just got out of there for a while. Laid low, like us. They could come here!"

"I tried. They're too stubborn."

From everything Kennedy had told her, that much seemed to fit. What she was wondering now was who, exactly, "they" referred to. After all, it wasn't every day that a person's soul could come out and talk to you. Yet she wouldn't have put it on Ruth the Soul to be any happier about leaving than the other two.

Ashlee had met Knuckles and Ruth only once, but she had been concerned about them since the moment she and Kennedy had fled the storage, the entire facility already engulfed in flames as they sped away on his motorcycle. He had reassured her then, too, but that didn't mean there was no room for doubt.

She liked them both, yet she couldn't help but feel a stronger pang of concern for Ruth. The one version of her, anyway. She had known who Ashlee truly was, and while she wouldn't reveal it when they met, for the sake of Ross's plan coming to fruition just as he had designed it, she had still managed to put Ashlee's mind somewhat at ease despite the danger she and Kennedy were in.

More than that, while Ashlee had felt powerless, hiding under Kennedy's wing until they could figure out what was going on, Ruth had made her feel special. She hoped to get to know her better.

"Alright. You should get back down there," Ashlee said, pulling her toothbrush and little travel tube of toothpaste from her bag. "The food will be here any minute."

"Lucky I'm back in, then," Kennedy said, surprised. "Unless you planned on answering the door like that."

Ashlee glanced over her still dewy skin and shrugged. "Save on the tip." When Kennedy frowned, she said, "Oh, lighten up, I'm kidding. You know, for a guy that's been twenty years old three different times, you can still shock like an old prude."

Kennedy thought that oddly fit, and remembered how he himself had made similar comparisons before. He was also reminded how his newfound youth, which Ross had bestowed upon him yet again, only moments before they had left him to come here, had been a significant topic of the day. One of those things that had prevented him from giving her the full details of their new digs. "I suppose I am, in a way. Don't forget, I'm actually ninety-four."

"Oh, I won't," Ashlee said, now with a mouth full of foam.

"And, uh…" Kennedy backed into the hall until only his head was peeking through the doorway, "…technically speaking, so are you." He ducked out just as the mini toothpaste tube whizzed past his head and over the railing to land on the first floor.

Ashlee spit in the sink and yelled, "There's no toilet paper, either, by the way." Then, pausing a moment, she stared at her body in the mirror. Unable to complain, she shrugged again and resumed brushing.

When Kennedy had been staying here previously, he had kept supplies to an absolute minimum, knowing that when the time came he didn't want to be stuffing all kinds of miscellany in his saddlebags or simply throwing it away, but he was almost certain he had left some toilet paper behind. He found it in the other upstairs bathroom, and dropped it unnoticed next to the door where Ashlee was now getting dressed, then headed back downstairs in time to see headlights coming toward the house, an indiscernible red, blue, and yellow sign sitting atop the car. He had no idea what Ashlee had ordered, but it suddenly seemed he could smell it.

To keep everything warm, he waited until she came down to even open the bags, but the logo had told him it was Thai and he remembered that, same as him, she liked things spicy. Her dark auburn hair was still wet because how could it not be, and she had it up in a ponytail presumably to keep her already damp shirt from getting completely soaked. Even her bare legs were still glistening. It seemed she was too hungry to let herself dry much at all, and he completely understood the feeling. It was the only reason he wasn't showering first himself.

"Good choice," he said.

"Wait till you see what I got."

He nearly gasped. "Don't tell me."

"Yep."

Gone were the days when he needed to baby his stomach. It wasn't so long ago he had even had to give up caffeine. Still, it had been fourteen years since the first time Ross had made him young again, and as Ashlee opened the bag it was the anticipation of his favorite dish that started him wondering how he had never sought it out in all the years since.

"Tom yum goong!" he said, peering through the clear plastic cover of the takeout bowl as Ashlee placed it in front of him.

"And all the yoozh," she said.

The usual was right. Pad thai, som tam, and even various bánh mì because, apparently, as he verified on the side of the bag now, the restaurant also served Vietnamese.

God bless those combination places.

He grabbed a set of the provided utensils, and peeled the cover off the bowl, smiling. It wasn't until he was getting ready to plunge his spoon in that a thought suddenly struck him.

It was odd that she had remembered.

Not because she outright shouldn't, but because it wasn't Ashlee who knew he liked Thai. It was Darling. The situation was unique, to say the least, and they were still getting used to it. In fact, they'd had more than one moment like this in the last twenty-four hours.

"Thank you both," he said.

Ashlee, looking slightly annoyed, shook her head, though she was still smiling. "I told you it's not like that."

"It's still funny."

"Yeah, and I bet it'll never get old."

By the time they finished, the street was even deader than when they arrived. Peeking through the heavy curtains, Ashlee found that all the houses had gone completely dark. So far as she could tell, at least. Aside from the single tall lamp at the entrance to the circle, there was no light spilling into the yards or onto the pavement. Not that she could have seen much of anything anyway, but then that was the point.

"So how long do you think until we hear from Ross?"

"Your guess is as good as mine. With his track record, I don't even want to think about it."

"But he wouldn't do that, would he? It's not like before. He asked for help. And it didn't sound like there was a lot of time."

He figured she was partly right. It wasn't like before. For decades, Kennedy had gone along, hoping to find her—Darling's—killer through the course of his work while Ross operated behind the scenes knowing eventually the lovers would drift back together and his plan would be complete. After secretly luring Ch'gal back so that Kennedy could finally confront him, then revealing, after so long, what he had really been up to, that was exactly how it had worked out. But it was apparently because of the expected timeframe itself that Ross, after Kennedy had first found him, had thought nothing of keeping him waiting years before making contact again. The question that had begun creeping into his head now was why they were waiting at all.

"Who knows? I told you, even if the Grille knows what happened at the motel, they definitely weren't expecting it. Not based on what Ch'gal said. It would have made more sense to attack right away, when they were surprised."

"Well, as little as I know about Ross, I think he knows what he's doing, don't you? I mean, if he doesn't, who does?"

"You've got a point there."

"So the question now is, what do we do in the meantime?"

Kennedy smiled, putting aside his confusion, as he was

getting ever more adept at doing when it came to Ross. He said, "You mean right now?"

Seeing his coy expression, Ashlee smiled back. They had only *just* been reunited, after all. "Oh, I know what we're doing right now."

Two

It turned out that when Kennedy had said there was no furniture, that wasn't entirely accurate. But neither was it accurate to refer to what they had slept on as "furniture." By the time they had gone to bed it had been a good twenty-four hours since either of them had slept, and their last attempt had been interrupted by an assault from a couple dozen beings from the Grudgeville Grille, and the alien formerly known as Ch'gal, who had killed Ashlee once already, back when she was only Darling, and was at it again now that he and seemingly everyone but her and Kennedy knew she was back. As a result, when Kennedy had suddenly produced two yellow self-inflating sleeping pads from out of nowhere, there wasn't enough of her still awake to question how. Or why the one was just her size.

It didn't come to her again when they awoke either, not least of all because there was a knock at the door.

"Ross!" Ashlee said. "Holy shit." She stared, both happy and surprised to see him. When a white flash circled in from behind his legs, she recognized what it was so fast she didn't have time to be startled. "And who is this?" Before Ross could answer, she was crouched in the doorway with two handfuls of fur, getting her face licked.

"He is Lab."

"Lab?" Ashlee said, incredulous. With Ross's thick Scottish accent she might have heard him wrong, but she didn't think she had. He was obviously a white Labrador, fur slightly off shade here and there, the rest of him nearly pale as snow.

"I am afraid he is incapable of naming himself," Ross said, "but as long as we can communicate, I cannot see fit to bestow one of my own upon him."

Ashlee had only met Ross two nights ago, yet even knowing how powerful he was, what he was capable of, she found herself entirely at ease around him. She suspected it was due in part to her long history as an incorporeal soul under his protection. That, and what he had done for them. Her and Kennedy. And the fact that Kennedy trusted him. The puppy couldn't have been more than a year old, yet was surprisingly well-behaved. Already, she couldn't help but see it as a reflection of his belonging to Ross.

She was still petting him when she finally realized she ought to invite them in. She stood, and was about to do so, but now the grin on Ross's face was so enthusiastic she might have found herself uneasy after all if he didn't also look so funny. "What?" she said, unable to avoid smiling herself even while thinking his expression was due to something more than just her being so enamored with his dog.

"I am pleased you are doing well," he said simply.

"Oh. Uh, thanks?"

Just then, Kennedy appeared behind her. "I wasn't expecting to see you anytime soon."

Considering how they had fled the storage—not even two days ago, though it felt like forever—clothing options were limited. On the cool floor, with no blanket, Ashlee had slept in her underwear and T-shirt, drawing enough warmth from Kennedy, even long after their lovemaking, to remain sufficiently comfortable all night. They usually wore nothing at all, but even Kennedy had found he needed to put his pants back on at least. If Ashlee didn't know better—that the words "Ross" and "sexuality" could not exist in the same sentence— she would have thought the odd moment that had just passed between them was about her attire.

She led Lab inside, and Ross followed, saying, "Then you

will need to tell Ashlee she was right. Now is not yet the time, but neither is it far."

Kennedy was no longer fazed when it was apparent Ross was reading his mind.

He did it freely enough that even Ashlee was already used to it, shutting the door behind them without questioning how Ross could know what she had said last night.

"Why?" Kennedy said. "Why is now not the time?"

"Kennedy…" Ross said, shaking his head slightly. As Ashlee brought Lab to sit against the living room wall, where she continued to pet him while she listened, Ross said, "Like you, Doge and his Council are confused as to why we did not mount an immediate attack, catching them off guard before they discovered what had happened at the motel. As predicted, they are now certain of how I plan to use you. They have greatly increased their forces inside the Grille, and indeed at every access point, not only the portal here on Earth, but those located elsewhere as well. Soon, they will again have agents out searching for you both. However, I am certain they will remain very far from here without the slightest clue where to look, and I will continue to monitor their movements to ensure that neither you nor your friends are in any danger besides. For the time being, just know that things are proceeding as necessary, and do not concern yourself with details that are better left to me."

Kennedy let out a sigh. This was in typical Ross fashion, and there never was much he could do about it.

But even while he was complaining internally, which he knew that Ross knew, Ross had addressed his concern for his friends before Kennedy had thought to mention it. There were benefits to his unconscious prying, too.

"What I can do," Ross continued, "what I came to do, other than implore you to be patient, is elaborate on the things we discussed at the motel."

"Alright."

"You will both remember how I told you that the Grille does not fear me so long as the Generator is operational."

"Yes," Ashlee said, scratching Lab's neck as Ross turned to her. He hadn't put it as a question, but it had been in response to one of her own questions that he had told them as much the first time.

"And that the Generator only prevents me from entering the Grille itself."

"Sure," Kennedy said. "What are you getting at?"

Ross smiled. "I told you at the motel that the Grille has been growing in both power and influence for some time, extracting money and resources on an ever-widening scale. But what I was referring to was their expanding exploitation of countless civilizations on other planets, in other solar systems, in other galaxies, throughout this universe, and many others. In reality, their presence and involvement on Earth is minor at best."

They were justifiably confused.

Then, Ashlee said, "Oh, I get it. They don't mess with Earth because you're here." The very night that she and Kennedy were reunited, it had quickly come up that Ross was effectively a pacifist. But funnily enough, it was only after the motel, and learning that she was more than who they thought she was, that Kennedy had explained the full context behind it. How after a relative eternity of destruction and death, Ross had sworn never to interfere with life again. And how he had been driven by regret to slightly modify that restriction. After witnessing her murder. "They don't know about your vow."

"Yes," Ross said. "But you are only partially correct. While my presence is certainly a deterrent, there are safeguards built into the Grille dimension that prevent something like an all-out invasion by another race, whether it be here or any other world where a portal exists. They are independent of my power, and therefore function even in my absence. However, barring that, the Grille has shown little interest in Earth for the simple fact that there are not enough natural resources to be extracted without notice. Especially when humans are still using so much. They of course tested the waters, but discovered quickly that the rewards were not worth the effort. Additionally, Earth is the only inhabited planet in the solar system, and while there is a finite number of portals leading to the Grille, many civilizations are no stranger to interstellar, even intergalactic, travel. With such access to the many worlds, their opportunities proved to be far greater elsewhere."

"Lucky for us, I guess," Ashlee said.

But Kennedy thought they were missing something. "But you can go anywhere you want, whenever you want. If they're too afraid of you to mess with Earth, even if that's only part of it, how did they ever get started anywhere else? I mean, even if your vow prevents you from just… wiping them out, why are they still able to use all these other portals?"

"I know what you are asking, Kennedy. While simultaneously welcoming visitors to this planet with my creation and safeguarding humanity against it, I find myself powerless to stop the Council's exploitation of the many worlds in its place. In a way, it is fortuitous that those few whose representatives make up the Council saw the benefit in spreading their pillaging over the others. Unless we act, there will be no end to it, but as yet they have been smart enough not to, as the story goes, kill their golden goose. Or in this case, geese.

"As for the portals themselves… Without getting into the finer details, I am unable even to prevent their usage, let alone close them, which is our ultimate goal. To do so, I will need access to both ends simultaneously, which of course is not possible so long as the Generator is up."

Kennedy still didn't get it. "But if you can travel anywhere at will, even without access to the portals they're using, couldn't you just—"

"Yes. You are correct. These last decades I have been focused primarily on the two of you, and in gleaning information from their agents merely to keep apprised of their activities, a fact, incidentally, that Doge and the Council already suspect, further explaining their behavior despite being ignorant of my vow. Perhaps it is selfish of me to enlist your aid in this now when I could simply disrupt their activities at every turn, but, in thinking of my salvation, I do not expect to remain here forever. To ensure that they are truly stopped, and the Earth, and everywhere else, can be safe, the Grille must be unmade. Is it wrong of me to think so?"

Kennedy suddenly felt like shit. They had been talking about this, limited though their contact had been, for as long as Kennedy had known him—the infinitely powerful Ross Wellington, seeking atonement for the sins of his past, salvation from a God he couldn't name any better than the things required to earn it. And yet here Kennedy was, practically accusing him of being selfish for trying, as though Ross should just race from portal to portal around the universe, or however many universes, for all eternity, slapping the Grille down wherever he found them, and be happy to do it.

"No, I take it back. Forget what I said, Ross. We owe you everything. I was just confused why they've been able to get away with it."

"You owe me nothing. But I appreciate your sense of obligation. It means I have done something right."

The silence that followed was Kennedy's fault, but Ross, at least, was once again smiling. Ashlee was still petting Lab, but now he lay across her folded legs as she watched him sleep. *When did he start calling him that?* Kennedy thought, realizing that Ross had never said, and proving, because he himself hadn't thought to ask, that he had forgotten what it was like to have a pet. *Poor little guy.* They had bonded years ago, a nighttime visit to the park, the very scene of Darling's murder, where Ross had finally explained the gruesome details behind it. He hadn't seen him since, or said anything when they arrived minutes ago, but it seemed to Kennedy he deserved a proper name.

It was this, thinking of the past and how this all started, on top of all the talk of the Grille, that made Kennedy suddenly remember where it more or less had for him.

"There's something else I don't understand," he said. "If the Grille doesn't really give a shit about Earth, how come you told me that night I tracked you down that they would 'play a part' before this was all over? You made it sound like they were going to be a problem one way or another, even though it was you who tipped them off about her." He thumbed at Ashlee. "And you never mentioned you would need anything from me, either. Just saying."

Ross nodded. "While it is true that it was my deliberately involving the Grille that first set them after you and Ashlee, even had they learned of Ch'gal's return and the reason behind it on their own, they would have permitted you no peace. And while they may have let you, both of you, alone once Ch'gal was no longer a threat, you still needed to see their true colors before I could ask for your help, as we have also discussed.

"The short answer is that I phrased it the way I did that night, and omitted any mention of needing your assistance, purely for simplicity's sake. But for reasons that will soon become apparent, I believe our actions even now were in a way destined. You were always going to have a part."

Slowly, that sank in. "You said soon. I take it you're not going to tell me now?"

Yet again, Ross only smiled.

"Fine. Then let's go back to these portals. Or one in particular." He was watching Ross's face. "That's why we're here, right? Why you sent us here? You said the city would be a good place to wait. Is it really that close? How can that be?"

"More excellent questions, Kennedy. For later. But do not

worry. You will understand all in due time."

Kennedy shook his head, but in the end relented. Not that he had a choice. "Whatever," he said. "My head still hurts from the other night anyway."

Three

Soon after Ross's departure, they had just finished eating when Ashlee returned to the living room with the intent of grabbing a change of clothes for a shower. It wasn't until she passed through the opening from the dining room and again saw everything lying there in the middle of the floor that she finally thought to ask. "So what's the story with the sleeping pads? I mean, why do you have two?"

Kennedy joined her. It was a reasonable question. And though she wasn't being accusatory, he couldn't resist. He smirked, and when her eyes went wide he knew it had worked. Suddenly she was wondering whether he had had other visitors.

"No, no," he said, already having taken it too far to back out without sounding desperate. She was glaring now, but he knew it wasn't because she didn't believe him. They liked to tease, and he had won this one. "It's because the first one I got felt a little small. By the time I realized it, I couldn't find the receipt, and the packaging was all torn up anyway. I honestly don't know why I hung on to it." Gritting her teeth, Ashlee still looked disgusted. "Lucky I did, I guess. You'd have been hurting this morning without it."

"Are you saying if you only had one you wouldn't have sacrificed yourself and let me use it?"

"Not necessarily. But you wouldn't have been very comfortable with me groaning in pain on the floor next to you all night either."

She grinned. "Well, that's what the bedrooms are for."

"Ouch. Heartless. I would say I deserved that if I didn't

think you meant it. Too bad, too. I just thought of something cool."

"Oh, tell me anyway," Ashlee pleaded now. "You know I was kidding."

"Fine," he said, surprising her when he began unbuttoning his pants. "Strip."

Soon they were in the pool, floating around on the pads wearing nothing but their sunglasses. When it boiled down to it, neither of them was modest enough to be concerned about the neighbors, even if they weren't in hiding, but with high fencing around the backyards, the faithful trees between the lots, and the fact that the nearest adjacent occupied house had no angle on them anyway, they didn't give it a thought. Not to mention, there was little else to do, and they had already done that. Several times since Ross had left, in fact. And the pads, on the one occasion they were employed, were serviceable for that, too.

"You know what I could go for right now?" Kennedy said.

Ashlee raised her head, her teeth suddenly gleaming like the rest of her save for the dark contrast of her tattooed arms. "If you're getting ready to say something about my pussy… It's been over an hour. What the fuck you waiting for?"

"No, I was going to say—" Now he looked at her over the top of his glasses. "Though, if you're offering…"

"I'm always offering."

"Well, I'm in the market."

When neither of them moved in the next moment, they just laid back again.

"Let's float a while longer," Ashlee said.

"Yeah. We really ought to shower first, anyway."

"What were you going to say, though?"

Kennedy thought about it. "I forget. Oh well. It'll come back to me."

The sun was high, and the sky was clear. The buoyancy of the sleeping pads was just enough to keep their bodies out of the water, so Ashlee started dipping her hand in and rewetting her warm skin while Kennedy dangled his feet below the surface.

After a moment, Kennedy opened his eyes again. "A part of me could get used to this."

"Which part?"

It seemed more rhetorical than anything, but it got him thinking. "I suppose the part that's been searching all these years, looking for Ch'gal without knowing it." It was only a couple of years ago that Kennedy had finally learned the identity of Darling's killer, and that he was a being unlike anything Kennedy had imagined. "I haven't had a lot of time to think since the motel. And now, helping Ross... It's not over yet, but I think maybe I could get used to not working so hard."

When it got quiet, Kennedy found Ashlee watching him, her hair slicked back, fresh droplets speckling her face, neck, and breasts. "We'll get through this," she said. "Ross knows what he's doing. I'm sure it'll be over soon."

"I hope you're right. On all counts," he added as he lay back down, though at the moment he was less concerned about whether things would happen safely than he was about whether they would happen soon.

"Well, he said he'd keep an eye on things for us, so there's no sense worrying about it until the time comes."

"I'm not worried. It would just be nice to have a bit more info. I'd like to know what I'm up against before I go in there."

"Before *we* go in there."

After a few seconds, now it was Ashlee who found Kennedy watching her. "I don't think so," he said.

"Excuse me?"

"You're not going to be anywhere near the place when this shit goes down."

Ashlee sat upright, swinging her legs over the side to face him. Kennedy thought it should have been tough for her to balance, her hands, hips, and butt bobbing underwater, the sleeping pad now forming a wedge that protruded from the surface. But by the look she was suddenly giving him, it was venom keeping her stable. "Who's going to stop me? You, fuckface? They wanted to kill me just to keep Ch'gal away. I have as much of a stake in this as you. More!"

He was slow to respond, so she laid back down. Now he spun his own pad toward her and sat up. "Look, I get it. I do. It's just… We don't know what it's going to be like in there, but it sure as hell isn't going to be easy. Even for me. It just never occurred to me you wanted to go in too.

"Well, it hereby occurs."

"Alright. I hear you. I mean, I still say no way, but—" She was glaring at him again, her sunglasses unable to hide it. "But there's no sense fighting about it now when we have no idea what it's going to entail or when it's going to happen."

"On that, we agree," Ashlee said.

It got quiet again. The idea of Ashlee accompanying him inside the Grille was about the least appealing thing he had ever heard, so naturally he had never imagined she would want to. Hell, she had to know that if Ross didn't need his help in bringing them down, even he wouldn't be going. As it stood, he was doing it more to ensure her safety than for anyone else's sake. If he knew the Grille would just leave them alone, he might be content to let the rest of the universe fend for itself.

She was lying there, her hands laced behind her head, her chest and arms already beginning to dry again. He had lost her once. If anything were to happen to her, he wasn't sure he had another lifetime of anguish in him.

Raising his right hand, he swung it outward, skipping it across the water, and splashed her entire left side.

Ashlee gasped, her breath catching. "You— motherfucker—"

When she saw him smiling, she launched herself toward

him. He tried to paddle away, but in two strokes she caught him in the shallow end of the pool and, dipping her shoulder under his hip, thrust off the bottom with her feet, tipping him over.

Now it was Kennedy, when he resurfaced, who was gasping for air. It was worth it, though, because now Ashlee was smiling too.

He snatched her up in his arms. "Our first fight. Sort of."

"Our first *new* fight."

"Weird."

Four

A moment later they were in the house, dripping, and pawing at each other like teenagers. The funny thing about it was that in terms of physical age Ashlee technically was one, and, even for as long as Kennedy had been around, he basically was too.

The sleeping pads were forgotten in the pool, but the carpet in the living room was soft and, from lack of use, virtually brand new. They would have done it outside, but water wasn't lube, and the stone around the patio was toasty from the sun, and too much for even the soles of their feet.

Groping and breathing heavy, Ashlee was pushing Kennedy backward toward the center of the room when she suddenly yelled, "Ow! Fuck!" Their guns were lying holstered on the floor next to where they had slept. While Kennedy had managed to miss them entirely, Ashlee had apparently kicked Penny Joy with her pinky toe so hard the weapon took a spin on the carpet. "I need to find a better spot for that."

Kennedy's .44 was specimen enough, being a large frame stainless steel revolver with a barrel over eight inches long, but Penny Joy, while shorter overall, was virtually a solid lump of copper, which made it even heavier.

"We could be stupid and put it in the safe," Kennedy said, alluding to the pointlessness of locking up one's weapons when at home. Thinking as he looked around, he even glanced upstairs, though there wouldn't be anything useful up there either. "If we could fashion a little table…"

"You have a safe?" Ashlee said.

When he saw she was serious, he was somehow even more

excited than before.

After she explained to him that she hadn't taken the tour last night—too tired and hungry to think about anything but a shower and food while he was on the phone—he led her to the opposite corner of the house to a room that was small enough for a spare bedroom or big enough for a large office. Against one wall, flanked on either side by built-in bookcases that were floor-to-ceiling and empty, was an enormous white gun safe.

Kennedy opened it, if only to prove it wasn't just a decoration, and the first thing Ashlee did was chuckle. "A gun safe, and no furniture," she said. Aside from a few sizable stacks of cash, it was chock-full and serving its purpose glowingly. "Honestly, I'm more surprised you have other guns. Somehow I've only ever pictured you with the one. Well, that and the ones on the bike."

Kennedy knew she was referring to his .44, and the rifle and shotgun stowed impossibly discretely on his motorcycle. "What can I say? Work is one thing, but shooting is fun. This is only here because I didn't really have room at the storage. I kept a few there, but that whole place was like a vault. They were just stuffed in a little cabinet behind the drafting table."

"Guess I never got around to digging through that one." She was teasing, reminding him how she had snooped while he was gone, and even found the little poem he had written for Darling. Or rather, her. That is, her when she was *only* Darling. It was only two nights ago that Ross had revealed the dichotomy, and it took some adjusting. She called herself Ashlee now, but she was technically both.

For his part, Kennedy thought he needed to remind her of the conditions of their bet. The shoot-off that had been intended not only to test her proficiency, but to get her, if he won, to use a weapon of his choosing, preferably lighter and less unwieldy than her massive Penny Joy. "Yeah, well I meant it when I said I was going to set you up with something more your size. We had some options. After I saw how good you were with yours, I guess I changed my mind."

"As I recall, you just wanted to kiss me," Ashlee said, reaching for him again.

She wasn't wrong. He had considered correcting her final shot, ensuring that she won. He hadn't, and in the end hadn't needed to. But admitting he had thought about it was enough. "As *I* recall," he said, now reaching in return, "a kiss was *your* idea."

"And you protested a whole ten seconds," Ashlee said, eyeing his lips.

Wrapping an arm around her waist and cupping one of her breasts with his other hand, he said, "Was it that long?"

They had switched places, Kennedy wanting to watch her as she surveyed the contents of the safe, Ashlee just as eager to feel the heft of the massive door. She had been slowly swinging it shut, her hand still on the handle, as they drew closer to one another. Now, as Kennedy pulled her down, she barely managed to engage the bolts before it all slipped from her grasp.

There was carpet aplenty in here, too.

Five

After all the traveling early yesterday, followed by sitting around all day and managing to eat only meagerly while trying to keep out of sight, they had been so tired and famished last night that after having dinner and nearly falling asleep during sex they got up late, had their surprise visit from Ross, and still finished their leftovers before lunch. As a result, they had found themselves famished again.

When Kennedy caught himself scarfing half of his second slice of pizza in one bite, he said, "We're going to get fat and sad if we keep this up. I'll order some real groceries tomorrow. Maybe some pans so we're not stuck trying to nuke everything."

Ashlee said, "And toilet paper. Toothpaste. Milk. Ooh, Oreos." She glanced at him. "I'll make a list."

Once they had one, Kennedy waited until Ashlee left the room to add a few additional items. Surprises. She would appreciate them, but in truth they would be as much for him as for her. They were in this together, after all, no matter that when the time came he was still intent on acting alone.

"You got any movies on the laptop?" Ashlee said, reappearing from the hall.

"No, but I'm sure we can find something." He was familiar enough with the concept of streaming to guess that much, but, unlike with the option to have virtually anything delivered these days, his lack of experience actually doing the thing had required Ashlee to introduce him to the phrase "free, with ads."

Back when he had apartments, he hadn't even owned a TV. No landline, no internet, and definitely no accounts tied to his address or name. Not even to the various pseudonyms he had used through the years for the sole purpose of walking among the living while keeping his true identity to himself. The storage had been a step beyond that, including a TV, Blu-ray player, and an assortment of movies. He had even put his stamp on the place—Ken, anyway, as in Ken's Mini Storage—but even that had been set up in such a way that it couldn't be traced back to *the* Kennedy James.

The real departure for him had been the properties in the cul-de-sac, where they were now, and which he had bought almost immediately after the land the storage was to be built on. Suddenly he was a property owner in a residential neighborhood, marking a complete departure from his previous modus operandi. But with a PO box, a gardener, a pool cleaner, and various other professionals who would regularly render their services without caring in the least to know who they were working for, he had once again managed to do it while keeping himself out of it. And now here he and Ashlee were, streaming movies on stolen Wi-Fi under the noses of neighbors who didn't know they had new neighbors. Far more preferable, as he had told her, than renting another apartment in a building of potentially nosy questions.

The pizza was cold by the time they finished it, which meant simply that they had gotten full but didn't stop. They had watched two movies, then three episodes of a series they eventually decided they just weren't into, before settling on a string of cooking videos that were somehow satisfying even though they were no longer hungry.

After a while, Ashlee burped. "Our bodies are one thing," she said, then pointed at the laptop. "How much of this before our brains are rotten, too?"

Kennedy was holding his belly. "We'll figure it out," he said. "It's not like we have much choice."

And in fact he had an idea of something they could be doing instead, but the thought of it was a little sickening in his current state.

Six

It was checkers, and after paying for expedited delivery they spent the next week with a kitchen full of groceries, all the miscellaneous essentials, and played game after game lying on their stomachs on the floor. Something that would have made them puke if they were still pounding pizza.

They had just finished a game when Kennedy got up to stretch his legs and heard the sound of one of the neighbors mowing the lawn again. Or rather having it done. The landscapers had been by here only yesterday, tending to all three of Kennedy's properties before noon, with no clue that one of them was suddenly occupied. Going to the window, he peeked through the curtains and found it was the same company, though based on how well they seemed to be keeping things it was no wonder others would want them too. After all, the sprinklers could only account for so much. It took real labor to do the rest. He knew the schedules for all of his hired help, so there weren't going to be any surprise visits, but suddenly he was curious to know whether anyone had adopted his chosen pool cleaner as well.

After fixing the curtains, he turned back around just as Ashlee was sitting up. Immediately, she winced, and started rolling her head around, stretching her neck. Then, in one of her new white tank tops—a pack of which had made it onto the list just in time before Kennedy placed the order—her hands began alternately poking and prodding her shoulders. She had requested only simple undershirts, and the sheerness of the fabric was revealing far more than the mere absence of tattoos anywhere but her arms. Kennedy couldn't help but note how sexy she looked, despite that she was in obvious pain.

"You want some help with that?" he said, behind her on his knees before she could answer.

She dropped her arms, letting his hands take the place of her own, and the second he touched her, she said, "Oh my god, I'm so tight."

Kennedy tried not to snicker. "That's great," he said, "but let's just focus on this massage for now."

At that, she burst out laughing, and he loved it. Remembering his own far poorer reaction when she had made a similarly perverted comment only a couple of weeks ago, it seemed she was rubbing off on him.

Afterward, Ashlee moved onto her sleeping pad with her sketchbook. Along with the checkers set, this was another of the surprises Kennedy had ordered, though it wasn't until afterward that he had begun to wonder just how it would be received. Surely, she would love it, he had thought. But which "she" was he more sure of? Once the delivery came and he was able to put the question to her, she had set to work on something while he watched. After only a few minutes, she said, "Huh. It's coming right back to me as Darling. And as Ashlee, it's nothing new."

With that out of the way, the next conundrum had been what the hell *he* was going to draw. It was her, Darling, after all, who had taught him, and until recently, and for the last nearly seventy-five years, it was her he drew. Or tried to. As it had turned out, part of Ross's plan to reunite them, or rather to give them the opportunity to find their way back to each other, involved Kennedy having no recollection of Darling's face. A face that Ross had ensured Ashlee shared. She was the same person. Presumably the same DNA, the same genes, all of it, though Ross hadn't spelled it out that way. He had simply said it was he who had ensured that Darling was the girl reborn, despite being carried by a different mother. And now

Kennedy knew and loved them both. He recognized their face again. Finally.

By the time they had figured all that out, it had seemed the only thing still missing—the one thing he didn't think to order—was cigarettes. Ashlee didn't *really* smoke, and he only did when he was drawing. But the only smokes he'd had burned up with the storage, and they apparently weren't something he thought he would miss. In fact, he didn't miss them now. Somewhere along the line he had picked up the habit, finding it soothed him, in some minor way, while he attempted and failed to draw his beloved. But once upon a time they had worked together like this, no additional ingredients required. And here they were once again.

It hadn't been so hard deciding what to draw after all, and between that, playing checkers, or watching something on the computer, they had spent each day in a similar fashion. This morning had been no different.

After a while, Ashlee said, "I forgot to ask you if there was any news?" her pencil still scratching away.

They hadn't heard from Ross again, so Kennedy had been doing the only thing they could: checking for any developments on the probable investigation into the fire at the storage. Admittedly, it was practically in the middle of nowhere, situated down the highway from the apparent junkyard that was Knuckles and Ruth's place, so, by design, it had never warranted much attention before. If anyone had enough motivation even to try figuring out the how or why behind what had happened, the most interesting fact would be the mystery of who owned the place. As well as why no one but Knuckles could ever complain about losing their stuff in the incident. As his one and only "customer," Knuckles had filled up a fair number of units with various crap from around his property just to appease Ruth, though he had since managed to fill the vacant spaces in the yard with a whole host of new crap. And since he cared far more about him and

Ashlee, and probably had no clue what precious miscellany he had lost besides, complaining was not something he was likely to do.

"Still nothing," Kennedy said, "but I'm not expecting much. On any given day, there's already too much shit going on for them to call it all news. That's good for us. Not that they could ever tie it back to me anyway, but I've always found that less attention makes for easier living."

Ashlee said, "You don't have to tell me twice," still hunched over her work.

More than once this week they had been talking only for him to look up and find her like that. Every time he did, it made him smile, reminding him of the time she was a little girl, drawing away in his apartment while he tried to sneak a peek at what eventually turned out to be a masterful portrait of him. She had been drawing it to thank him for saving her, at the time temporarily, from the stepfather who was molesting her. At that thought, his smile would disappear again.

"What are you working on?" Kennedy said.

Then, as though she was reading his mind, "Maybe it's a surprise." When she faced him, she was smiling now.

There was a time when Ashlee had seemed to know things. Things she had no way or reason to know. It wasn't like with Ross, who could reach into your brain and literally see what you were thinking, know what you were going to say before you did. It was in the details. She would seem to have information she shouldn't. About Kennedy. About the quest he was on. And now they knew why.

Part of it was her exposure to Ross. Buried within her were memories, feelings, about the time she had spent with him. The decades before he had brought her back. She was only a soul traveling under his protection, but the things the experience had apparently impressed upon her had informed and aided them both in mysterious ways ever since.

The other part of it, as strange as it still seemed, was simpler to explain. She had known things about Kennedy from the very beginning, not only real things he had done, but who he was and the kinds of things he *would* do, because she wasn't only Ashlee. She was also Darling. And before Ashlee was ever born, before even her mother had been born, Darling had known Kennedy better than anyone.

It added up, at any rate. But even after explaining away the reasons behind her seeming to just know things, the success in her smile now wasn't the first time in the past week that Kennedy had been reminded of how Ashlee Carter had always been.

"Is it?" he said, meaning a surprise.

"No. I'm actually just drawing this room with furniture."

"Can I see?"

"I'm not sure you want to."

Kennedy was perplexed. It sounded like she was concerned with the quality of her work. Ridiculous. "Is it... bad?"

"No, it's just once you see it there's no going back. We still have to sit here on the floor knowing what we're missing."

"I'll risk it," Kennedy said. "It's not like I've never been comfortable before."

Ashlee held up the sketchbook. Unfortunately, she was right. The image might as well have been of him lying on a beach with a drink in his hand. It was only a moment before the inflated, bubbled surface of the sleeping pad reminded him where he was, but the initial impression must have shown on his face. Ashlee said, "Told you." Picking up her pencil, she went back to work. "I've been thinking how stupid it was we didn't have Ross conjure us up a couch or something at least."

"I'm not sure it works like that."

"Well, I'd give anything to ask."

Seven

It took little effort to feel them. The insects above and below the ground. The birds high in the sky. Fish, in the nearest body of water, though no such body was anywhere near here. He could feel every Grille agent currently assembled before him, and even those few otherwise spread across the Earth. The ones he was watching now had instructions to report any sign of himself or "the hitman," as they often referred to Kennedy. Like so much else, these were things Ross was able to know, along with the simple fact that there was nothing they could do to hinder him here, outside the Grille dimension. What he could not know, thanks to the Generator, were the thoughts and actions of those inside.

They had the portal now enclosed within a small warehouse. He had taken care to put it underground, buried beneath the desert in an area that could not possibly be discovered by accident, while still allowing convenient egress and ingress for those weary travelers who had already come so far, and would have farther still to reach civilization. The area was now excavated, stairs and even a freight elevator, making the portal's usage all the easier, yet all the more exposed if not for the precautions they had taken.

Vehicles and equipment were stowed at one end of the building for those agents with business on Earth. It was only a matter of time before they would be out searching for Kennedy and Ashlee, but currently every additional agent not already amassed inside the Grille was on guard outside this very building. And they numbered in the dozens. On a normal day, one might think it was a private garage of some kind with a small, dedicated security detail. Now it looked more like an industrial wedding reception. And in the heat and dust, of which Ross was only intellectually aware, not a pleasant one.

He, of course, did not have to be present to observe the activity here, but he had nowhere else to be. Yet after several days of watching and learning, he had nothing more to tell Kennedy and Ashlee than he had when he left them at the cul-de-sac. For all the pain and sorrow his friends had endured along their journey, he could not help but feel satisfied that his plan had come together thus far, considering that in the beginning he had known scarcely what he was planning for. But the fact that he had gleaned nothing of relevance from those he observed spoke more to the idea that they were not privy to the information than it did that Doge and his Council simply had no idea what to do. Even Ross Wellington could not know everything, a fact that was becoming increasingly evident the more he tried. At least where these events were concerned.

The agents milling about before him had been rotating in shifts since the previous morning. It was the only new development to speak of, and one that Ross *had* fully predicted. So much so that even before they began to do it he had incorporated the feature into his plan: creating a diversion at the portal. This would ensure that the agents outside would send word inside that something was happening, at which time he would simply detain them, prevent their reentry, to relieve Kennedy of the reinforcements. The additional agents outside the portals elsewhere would be another story, but even should they try to interfere, their greater numbers would likely make little difference in time to disrupt Kennedy's efforts against whatever those already amassed inside would throw at him. As long as he brought the Generator down quickly, which Ross was reasonably hopeful that he could. Kennedy could.

If everything went according to plan, there was even a

chance, however slight, that those inside would be staring in vain at the portal right up until Kennedy succeeded. He had been right to ask how it was that the portal was so close, but the answer warranted more explanation than the time Ross had been willing to devote when he did. As did the fact that, when the time came, this would not be his entry point besides.

Eight

The conference room was decidedly less occupied these days, the core group never wavering while the majority of others now claimed to have more pressing work back home. This, and that after satisfactorily beefing up security both inside the portal and at the many locations outside, it had become something of a waiting game in which none had expected to be waiting so long.

That it had, but it wasn't why they were gone. They were gone because they were cowards.

Agents had seen nothing of note since they had truly started watching. Not that they necessarily would unless Wellington wished it, but even if his intent was to deposit Kennedy James on their doorstep, it remained a wonder he hadn't done so already.

It was unlikely, at the very least, that Wellington was intending for the hitman to infiltrate from anywhere other than Earth. Moving the portal all those years ago might have been meant to throw them off, but it would hardly seem worth the effort considering the resistance they would have waiting inside. That they did have waiting inside. Especially now, with the time he had given them. Still, it might have been useful to put a Generator *outside* each of the portals as well, if only to provide a greater buffer. That is, had they known in the first place that Wellington wouldn't be working alone.

Hindsight, Doge thought, though it seemed that what they did know didn't amount to much either. Sitting at the head of the table, several empty chairs pushed all the way in, more, still, sitting vacant around the dark edges of the room, he used a lull in the discussion to silently consider the main points yet again.

Wellington couldn't penetrate the Grille while the Generator was up. It must also be true that he couldn't be everywhere at once. Yet in all the time the Generator had been operational, he hadn't interfered with their outside operations or agents *anywhere*, in the least. And while Doge had assumed that Wellington had intended to somehow use Ch'gal to circumvent the Generator technology, Ch'gal had apparently been of no real use to him personally, bringing little sense to the idea of letting him live all those years ago, if not less for suddenly wanting him dead now. And that was to say nothing of why he had used the girl to lure him back in the first place.

It was possible, however unlikely, that he and the hitman had somehow missed their initial chance, and that the heavier presence outside the portal had been sufficiently discouraging of a direct assault since. But the dots that could not be connected kept leading him back to a thought he had dismissed in the early morning hours after the events at the motel, and an idea that had begun to form only today, under the premise that waiting any longer was an invitation for Wellington to make a move.

They needed to act, and to do that they needed to know what they were missing.

Unfortunately, it would not be that simple.

"I propose we go on the offensive," he announced, the various whispers around the room ceasing as all the quiet conversations rejoined the one. "If we do not, we are merely allowing things to play out as Wellington wishes."

"But what can we do, Kalar?" Fio said, his eyes no more desperate than the discussion had been of late. "Without Wellington feeding us information, to his own benefit or not, we have as much hope of finding the hitman as we do of understanding what they are waiting for in the first place."

"I still say it's the girl," Ceyon said before Doge could

respond. "Gurba did say they were being intimate when they found them at the motel."

"'Fucking like bunnies' was how he put it," someone added, drawing a gaze from Qazaen and others, and setting a blush to the olive-complected cheeks of young Halan. The relative innocence of Thule's protégé was always on display, but the events of late seemed to have triggered a heightened anxiety in the lad, and had even drawn out a sort of protective instinct from none other than Qazaen herself.

Doge could only nod. "Yes. It is obvious that Gurba's work was subjecting him to too much contact with humans in general."

"But we have been through this," Fio said. "You cannot believe that is a factor. New lovebirds, reluctant to put themselves in danger? If that was a likely outcome, surely Wellington never would have thought to use them."

Ceyon said, "I might agree, if we truly understood anything at all. As it stands, her return makes as little sense as why Wellington, after all this time, would suddenly want Ch'gal dead."

And they had been through all of that so many times, Doge was already dreading what he knew he must do.

"You are both right," he cut back in. "In one sense or another. But the fact remains that if we want to survive this we must take the initiative. We will draw the hitman out. Confront him here, as they are surely planning themselves, but on our own timetable, not theirs. Incite him to act. Catch him ill-prepared, and off guard, where Wellington cannot follow. Enraged, not strategic. That is our best course."

"But what about Wellington?" Fio said. "Things are not like before. He has left us alone all these years, and we chalked it up to his apparent desire to remove himself from our affairs for good, if not simply to keep tabs on our agents to learn what he could. But who is to say his motivations haven't changed now that the time has apparently come for him to employ the hitman? We have no reason to believe he will allow us an inch of progress. Anything we do, he will see it coming!"

Fio, of course, was correct. And this was the part that Doge knew would not be so easy—a private venture birthed of their endlessly frustrating circumstances. "Perhaps not," he said. "Not if we do it right."

Nine

After another week, they had lapsed into a routine of finishing the night with watching something on the computer. For the most part, it was things they had seen before, if only so the predictability would translate into sleepiness. And in light of their combined history, it had to be something from either the golden age of Hollywood or the last twenty to thirty years.

Kennedy was sitting on his sleeping pad, which he had folded against the wall. Ashlee's had sprung out straight when she got up to use the bathroom, and had sailed too far away for Kennedy to reach. He had been waiting about five minutes when he heard a flush, followed by a hasty spray of water from the sink and the hiss of the toilet tank refilling.

A second later, Ashlee appeared from the hall, stopping across the room as soon as she saw him. "Hey, what's the date?" she said unexpectedly, not moving, as though she'd be off again once she had an answer.

Kennedy had no idea. He also hadn't put his watch back on after doing the dishes. "Hm, funny enough, I couldn't tell you if we didn't have it right here." He leaned forward to check the laptop. "It's the fifteenth. What, you have an appointment or something?" he said, smiling.

"No, I just... Just wondering, is all." And it seemed like she actually was, standing there thinking about... something. Then her face made a sort of wince, and as she stared blankly toward the dining room one of her hands moved slowly to her bladder.

It probably only seemed like her bladder, though. A little

constipation would explain why she had been gone a whole five minutes, but *only* five minutes. Long enough to try, but maybe not enough to finish.

No matter, he thought. If she wanted to try again, she wouldn't hesitate to tell him. Neither Ashlee nor Darling had ever been bashful in that department.

"You coming, or what?" he said.

She snapped out of it when he started patting his sleeping pad, telling her to rejoin him.

Taking his cue, she said suddenly, "Hey, can we go out tomorrow? Even just to that big gas station we saw on the way in, or something? I've got to get out of the house."

He watched as she slid her pad back against the wall, folding it and holding it in place underneath her as she sat. The whole time she did it, she watched him in return. Almost hopeful. Not that he could blame her. "I guess so," he said. It was a calculated risk, but not completely unwarranted. "A quick trip will do us both some good. It's actually been bugging me that I didn't fill up the bike when we first got here anyway. It's no good sitting like it is if we have to run again."

"Good," Ashlee said, though with no real appearance of relief, almost like she wasn't buying it. As she faced the computer again, waiting for him to resume the movie, he figured that at this point they had been here long enough, and talked so much about staying out of sight, that maybe she had to see it to believe it.

Ten

Kennedy made good on his promise, not that Ashlee had doubted it. She did, however, know that even with Ross supposedly keeping tabs on any Grille agents who might by now be out looking for them, Kennedy wasn't keen on inviting trouble. Going out was bad enough, even if it was marginally necessary, but letting her out of his sight was a step too far. That's why she waited until he had started pumping, his attention still on the opening of the bike's large tank, before she made for the door.

"Hey, where you going?" he said to her back.

"Snacks," she said, stopping only a second. "I'll be quick." He didn't look happy, but what was he going to do?

After Kennedy insisted that they come early, barely after sunrise, they had arrived just as two cars drove off, seconds apart, in different directions, leaving only a truck driver and his rig under the tall canopy by the diesel pumps. For the moment, Ashlee was the only customer inside.

First, she found the aisle for what she was really looking for. Every place had one. The stuff you were supposed to buy at a "real" store, but maybe you're traveling, or you forgot, or it's late night and nothing else is open. For her, it was because she knew Kennedy would have been much less receptive to venturing any farther than right about here. And, because she remembered the place looking so big, they were bound to not only have such an aisle, but for theirs to be bigger than most.

With that business done, and it being a gas station, the snacks were just about everywhere else. Even so, she didn't have time to be picky, grabbing a bag here, a bar there, and while Kennedy could be seen still working the pump outside, she made her way to the counter.

She set the first item down, which the cashier immediately scanned, then plopped down the rest as she grabbed it back, quickly tearing it open. Sliding the contents into her front pocket as the cashier finished bagging the snacks, Ashlee pushed the now empty packaging toward him and said, "Can you throw that away for me?"

He picked up the box and looked at it. Just as she was beginning to silently accuse him of judging her, he said, "Thought I ought to check the expiration. I don't remember ever selling one of these."

Ashlee took the bag and threw a couple of bills down on the counter. "Yeah," she said. "Lucky me."

She walked out just as Kennedy was hanging up the pump. When he saw her, he popped open his saddlebag, and said, "You know, I had to go in there anyway. It's not like I have a credit card."

She did know, which was why she had gone alone, and why she was already munching on something. "I couldn't wait," she said, now handing him the bag in her hands.

Kennedy gave her a look. "For a Slim Jim?" She shrugged, still chewing. "Then I guess we better get some on the list."

Eleven

After he paid, they headed straight back. Ashlee was still quiet, but she did seem somehow refreshed, as though the air was doing her some good. He made a conscious note that going forward they should at least try to spend more time around the pool. That is, the part of him that wasn't merely dreading the idea of this going on much longer.

They managed to sneak back down the street and into the garage, the neighbors, if they were up and still home, going about the normal routines that presumably kept them inside until the coffee kicked in and the kids were fed. After closing the door and retrieving Ashlee's haul from his saddlebag, Kennedy put the bike into motorcycle mode once again.

The instant they got in the house, Ashlee made a beeline for the bathroom. It was no wonder why. Not that he was above craving junk food, but he'd be damned if *his* first meal of the day was going to be some impulse buy from a gas station.

Minutes later, he was in the kitchen reheating leftovers when he heard, from behind the solid wood door and down the hallway that connected both the dining room and living room, a muffled, yet resounding, "Shit!"

After a while more, there were two clearly extended flushes, Ashlee holding down the handle to inject extra water. Then the door opened, and she appeared once again from the hallway, standing in the dining room looking as chagrined as he figured she ought to.

From his place at the counter, he said with a smile, "Probably that Slim Jim."

"What?"

"It sounded like a fight in there."

"Oh. Yeah. Doodie calls."

"Is something up?" Kennedy said.

"Me? I'm fine. You know how it is. It's gonna be a few minutes before my butthole feels like normal."

Twelve

Doge sat in his office with the door closed, his elbows on the desk as he slowly massaged the swollen flesh at the base of his horn. In addition to keeping a heavier presence outside the portals, they were now engaged in an aggressive search for the hitman. As before, he and the Council had no expectation of actually finding him, but it might serve, both aspects, to convince Wellington it was all they could think to do. If Wellington's objective at present was to continue trying to glean information from any agents in the field, they had to believe he would only welcome more of them. In the meantime, Doge's theory went that as long as he continued to keep his plan to himself, the presence of more agents wouldn't benefit Wellington in the least, while those few who were dispersed elsewhere, continuing to go about their daily routines, would further serve the illusion that nothing else was afoot.

He could hope, at any rate. He would have liked nothing more than to put all this business out of his mind, but the fact remained that they didn't know what they didn't know. And with as clueless and desperate as they were finding themselves lately, how could they pass judgement on the significance of such details? Common sense dictated that whether they could truly ever thwart the grand plans of the great Ross Wellington or not, their own ignorance could only be to his benefit. He believed it with the same conviction that had led him to impress upon the Council their need to go on the offensive. Yet it wasn't until Ceyon, in private, immediately following that meeting, had passingly broached the subject of Kennedy

James' first direct contact with the Grille that Doge suddenly knew how to begin.

It had to do with the matchbooks. Created by Wellington, invariably possessing some magic they couldn't begin to understand, a person needed one just to call into the Grille dimension in the first place, which the hitman had done. Their concern over him had been nearly nonexistent before then, and even until recently, the various minor ways in which his work would sometimes impact their activities having never been significant enough for them to risk exposing themselves in order to address it. Or for them to suspect that it was anything but coincidental. Now that it had become apparent that he was in fact Wellington's pet, Doge wasn't so sure. And when Ceyon had inadvertently reminded him of the matchbooks, Doge had become all the more suspicious of Kennedy James' having come to possess one. This had further reminded him of a man named Alfonse Guiturro.

Guiturro was a well-known broker rumored to have worked extensively with Kennedy James, and it was known that he possessed a matchbook because he had done some digging of his own, leading the Council at one time to eliminate three known subjects of his inquiries, sufficiently dissuading him from digging further. After learning of Guiturro's apparent execution through the usual course of things, accompanied by a new rumor that it was the famous hitman himself who had done it, the timing of a phone call from a new contact on the outside was too perfect but to assume exactly how the matchbook had changed hands. They did pop up from time to time, but it was exceedingly rare, so they had taken it for granted that Kennedy James now possessed the matchbook from almost the moment the front manager had reported his original call to the Council. Now that they knew the hitman and Wellington were linked, there could be no doubting it.

Yet it was merely by strange coincidence, it seemed, that

the hitman had ever gotten it. Doge had confirmed that Wellington was unable, in that obnoxious, fury-inducing way he used to when they were face-to-face, to read his thoughts over the phone, whether due to the Generator being active or the communication technology itself, by stating something that escaped Wellington's grasp, finding him unable to catch his meaning—that by concluding their business with the humans, referring to both Kennedy James and the girl, they may finally be rid of him as well due to the simple fact that he'd *had to* call, which meant the Generator was truly working. As a result, Doge also knew that he had been successfully coy with him, acting almost surprised that the hitman had a matchbook, as though the Council didn't already know. Admittedly, that part was just for fun, but whether Wellington believed it or simply wasn't letting on that he knew better, in the moment even Doge had forgotten the truly odd way in which it had come to pass: Despite it being obvious, between his extended longevity and the events at the motel, that Wellington had been grooming the hitman for his own purposes for some time, it hadn't come from him.

Also strange, once he had begun to think about it, was that twice now the hitman had referred to himself as having "found" the matchbook. The second time could merely have been a reminder, but it was odd that he would have expected them to know who was calling even then. After all, they had figured it out themselves. Not once had he said. It was possible Wellington had told him they knew.

Ultimately, the odd circumstances mattered very little. After a bit of research—it helped to know who to contact, even if they didn't know precisely who was asking—he had confirmed what he and the Council had heard all along. That Kennedy James had, in fact, done a great deal of work with the late Alfonse Guiturro. An exclusive relationship, going back many years. The hitman's reputation had long preceded him—almost too long—but it wasn't until they had tied him to Wellington that they believed it could be the original man, one and the same, who had been working all that time. It was out of sheer curiosity that Doge had suddenly wanted to know just what kind of timeframe they were talking about. And what he had found had not only led him frustratingly back to one of the same old questions he was tired of asking, but had very nearly thrown him into a fit.

From the moment they had learned of the girl's return, heralding a renewed threat from Wellington, there had existed a deeper aspect to all this that they just couldn't put their finger on. What had begun as a facetious assumption—that Wellington had lured Ch'gal back, after all this time, merely to kill him—had proved to be true. Yet he had involved the hitman, whom he had been grooming for reasons which only now seemed obvious, and the girl, apparently resulting in some romantic connection, when he could simply have dispatched Ch'gal himself at any old time he pleased, including decades ago, when he had hunted him down to retrieve that very same girl's soul. The same old annoying question that had come back to him was what any of this had ever had to do with Ch'gal. But what had set his forehead to throbbing was what he had discovered after some further research.

He now knew, without a doubt, that the infamous Kennedy James had been active even back then.

If that wasn't enough, there was a clear logical disconnect that stood out now as well: If Wellington had been planning this from the beginning, since the days of Ch'gal's original fiasco, it meant that he knew the Council was attempting to bar his return. Yet if he had known that, if he had known that they were developing the Generator technology, let alone that they would eventually succeed, he could have simply prevented it. And though it did offer some explanation into why Wellington had moved the portal at that time as well, to which they had always struggled to assign some motivation, it made the idea that he simply could have stopped them and hadn't all the more confounding.

Dropping his hands, Doge folded them across his lap as he sat back in his chair. As little as any of it made sense, he had reason to feel satisfied. The Council had not only acquiesced to the idea of his developing their offensive plan on his own, but they had believed him when he said that as long as they could put an end to all this and come out intact on the other side, it didn't matter whether they ever got to the bottom of it. Both were important, but they had to believe the second point for the same reason they needed to trust him with the first: because it would facilitate what he was going to do next.

During that same call with Wellington, Doge had also asserted that the phones worked independently of Wellington's power. Wellington hadn't outright confirmed it any more than he had anything else, but considering he hadn't caught on to Doge's meaning concerning the Generator being functional, Doge, by extension, took that to mean that he was unable to monitor activities inside the Grille by *any* means. Strange, considering the way he had built it, its potential both forever limited, it would seem, by his infatuation with Earth, yet infinitely upgradable, even in his absence, allowing them to keep pace with changing human technologies, however primitive, in this environment where only they worked best. They still didn't understand where the electricity came from. But who cared as long as they had internet?

Now more than ever, coordinating their offensive meant finally answering the questions that had been plaguing them from the start. And now that he knew Wellington would be none the wiser as long as he kept his thoughts inside his own head, no more capable of gleaning anything from the Grille agents coming and going at the portal than by electronic means, he was free to pursue both avenues to his heart's content.

Thirteen

Ashlee had apparently been up already because when the *knock! knock! knock!* woke him, Kennedy was the only one surprised. Not that she seemed raring to go, or anything, but lucid enough as she rose to answer it. The soft glow coming from the patio off the dining room confirmed that it was, in fact, morning.

Now that they had a blanket, they were back to sleeping like normal. Ashlee might have thrown something on first had he not reassured her already that unless they were out in the street the neighbors couldn't really see down here anyway. Or if it could have been anyone other than who it must be.

Ashlee swung open the door and said, "Good morning, Ross," before moving back to let him in. After seeming a bit off since their all too brief and unstimulating trip to the gas station barely twenty-four hours ago, Kennedy thought it was nice to hear, whether for Ross or their now mutual furry friend, a hint of enthusiasm in her voice.

If Ross noticed her appearance, he didn't let on. Nor did he seem to notice as Kennedy threw off the blanket and began searching out his underwear. In fact, only Lab offered any kind of acknowledgment as to their nudity, taking the opportunity to lick Ashlee's bare knee in the brief moment before her hand reached his head.

When he started toward Kennedy next, Ashlee again shut the door, and as she moved casually to retrieve her own clothes, Kennedy said to Ross, "To what do we owe the pleasure? Things are coming along, I take it?"

"No developments on my end," Ross said. "But I thought

it was time for a visit."

Kennedy glanced at Ashlee as she was slipping her second leg into her panties. "No developments?"

Ross shrugged. "Not on my end."

Suddenly Ashlee, bent over and pulling on her waistband, froze like she had finally heard him and now understood why Kennedy was disappointed. That, or she was just realizing she was naked and actually cared, which was highly unlikely. In fact, rather than respond to the annoying fact that it seemed Ross had nothing new to report, or pick up the pace to get dressed and cover herself, she looked almost... nervous.

Kennedy said, "You alright? You seem—" When her gaze shifted, it hit him. "Ahh, I get it. You thought I was going to forget." He turned to Ross. "She's worried you're going to take my side when you hear—" Then he caught himself. "Not that you wouldn't already know, I guess. You're just being polite."

When Ross only smiled, Kennedy proceeded to explain about the argument they'd had shortly after Ross had last left them. How they had disagreed about whether, when the time came, she should accompany him inside the Grille. After all, Ashlee couldn't read minds any more than he could, and it was only fair that she be reminded of exactly what Kennedy was arguing before Ross told her he agreed.

He stated his case, Ashlee staring intently at Ross the entire time while the latter politely listened.

When Kennedy was finished a moment later, Ross faced both of them, a little smirk on his face, and said only, "I will not pass judgement. Of all people, I am sure the two of you can reach an understanding with which you will both be content."

Kennedy wondered if there was a word for being disappointed by your expectation of feeling relief from your disappointment. He came up with nothing. And yet with those few words Ross had managed to make everything seem... as settled as it could be. For now.

Ashlee continued getting dressed, and Kennedy followed, immediately going back to what Ross had opened with. "So what do you mean there's no developments?"

"There is nothing significant to speak of. As expected, the Council has enacted a widespread search for you, but they are very far from here, and I have constant knowledge of their whereabouts. Even had you not done so well in procuring this property, Kennedy, they would have no hope of finding you.

"As for my surveillance... Since the Generator prevents me from reading anyone inside the Grille, my only option remains to monitor those emerging from the portal and moving about freely outside. Thus far, what I have found is more curious than anything."

"And what is that?"

"They all seem to be experiencing a certain level of increased frustration, if not impatience, coming from their superiors. It seems that Doge is withholding something from the rest of the Council. Likely, he has learned that their numbers constitute too many to keep secrets, and now thinks it better to work alone."

"So they're worried what he's up to," Kennedy said.

"Yes."

"But you're not?"

"Not significantly."

Kennedy stared blank-faced for a moment as though certain there was going to be more. When he realized there wasn't, he said simply, "Why?"

"Because it was never my intent to be reactionary. We are executing a plan that was defined long ago, and the end is nearly here."

Oddly, at that Kennedy felt equally exasperated and relieved, and glanced to Ashlee to see whether she was having the same reaction.

When he couldn't read her, he turned back to Ross. "Then

why the visit?"

Ross smiled. "If only to break up the monotony for us all, would that be enough?"

Kennedy was still at somewhat of a loss. But despite himself, he could find no reason to object, either. "Sure."

They then proceeded, in a way he would never have thought possible, to hang out.

Apparently, Ross had loosened up somewhat over the years, though Kennedy had rarely had occasion to test it. Until a few weeks ago, the guy had shown up for two brief visits in the last fourteen years, and it seemed that on each occasion, for all Kennedy had learned, they had still barely strayed from the matters at hand. Suddenly the conversation was loose and, strange as it would have seemed given the frustration Kennedy felt at times during all of their interactions, almost entirely enjoyable. Ashlee, too, seemed to find a lighter mood again after their veritable tease of an excursion yesterday, and when they managed to avoid wandering back into the territory of what they knew was coming, what they were preparing for, they were all quick to laugh.

For all his wisdom and power, and his ability to know and influence and predict virtually anything he wished, Ross Wellington had remained socially awkward until this very moment, it seemed, if for no other reason than lack of practice. He still hadn't gotten in the habit of using contractions, which Kennedy had always thought made him sound excessively formal, despite his thick accent. But finally, for one solid afternoon, he was practically human.

They talked about little things. Little, because they didn't matter so much anymore. One was the storage. Not that what had happened there was a little thing, but when Ashlee mentioned her surprise about the cul-de-sac, how Ross hadn't mentioned this location, specifically, the night at the motel, and how Kennedy had chosen for them to remain hidden at the storage when they were first reunited rather than coming here, Ross pointed out something about the former location that Kennedy had never considered. Once Kennedy had saved Ashlee from her abusive stepfather, even knowing he couldn't return to the apartment where they had met, he still had been reluctant to leave the city of Darling's murder because it was there that he had always expected to find her killer. Unbeknownst to him, part of the reason he was ultimately okay relocating was because he was again being drawn to her, Darling, now Ashlee, and now in the custody of her aunt, even while he believed it would also help him stay away from her, keeping her safe. He had chosen to build the storage and remain there, but in the end he was once again rather close.

Kennedy then proclaimed that Ross had blown his mind, though he barely reacted at all. Apparently, he was finally getting used to it.

Another thing, when it came around, was Ch'gal's power, and why he had pursued them to the motel on a motorcycle instead of simply teleporting to where he needed to be. It was because his power didn't work like that, Ross explained. It was unlike Ross's own. Ch'gal could move between dimensions, as Kennedy had witnessed, and even from a geographical location on a planet in one dimension to the same location on a corresponding, or sister, planet in another dimension, but he could not truly teleport, meaning choose where he would land, and therefore had to travel terrestrially the old fashioned way upon arrival. As it was, he hadn't even come via the Grille, which would have landed him very near to where he needed to be, because he apparently hadn't been on a planet with a portal, or close enough to one that it would have saved him any time.

"Not that he needed it," Kennedy said, Ross's explanation leading him organically to a follow-up question. Namely, how Ch'gal had found them so quickly the second time around, after Ross had stopped hiding them—their souls—from Ch'gal's detection, when Kennedy and Darling had already been engaged by the first time Ch'gal came around.

"Because love grows," Ross said simply. "I have told you both how rare you truly are. I had never seen such a connection before, nor have I since. In fact, the others in his collection—all those souls you freed when you destroyed him—were unique to him for entirely different reasons, and yet rare enough that he had not collected another in all the time I was tracking him. But just because you are soul mates does not mean your connection was immediately as strong as it would eventually become. It is probable he was biding his time at the start. And of course once he had *you*," he said to Ashlee, "and I knew what he was, I made sure he was unable to find *you*," he told Kennedy, "as I have said."

Kennedy hadn't thought about those others since later that same night, describing to Ashlee how they had risen from Ch'gal's corpse, but to hear Ross describe it now made more sense of it. As old and evil as Ch'gal had been, apparently he was also very picky. It seemed he could afford to be.

Pointing out that it was lunchtime, Kennedy refused to break at the risk of Ross suddenly feeling less generous, and insisted they all move to the kitchen to continue the conversation while he made something. As far as he knew, Ross didn't eat. Ever. So as Kennedy moved between the fridge, pantry, and stove, and Ashlee sat on the counter, Ross... Perhaps not to distract them by standing in the middle of the dining room while they spoke, Ross bent his knees and reclined back on... nothing.

For a moment, Kennedy couldn't imagine anything more distracting, and with a look attempted to confirm for Ashlee that he had never done that before.

"Not that I want to keep thinking about Ch'gal," Kennedy said quickly, trying to ignore the unusual, "but what you said last time about me having a part reminded me of something you said at the motel that makes even less sense now. At first, we thought the Grille was after us for my digging around trying to find Darling's killer, when all they really cared about was stopping Ch'gal, who wanted her." He indicated Ashlee. "You said they didn't even know about our past relationship."

"That is correct," Ross said.

"So then how did they even know who I am? I mean, on the phone, Doge talked about my 'infamous reputation,' but—"

"I appreciate your modesty, Kennedy," Ross said, now smiling, "but, simply put, you have been far too prolific to go unknown, even to an entity as far removed from Earth as the Grudgeville Grille and its governing Council. As I have said, they have blessedly little interest in Earth on the whole, but for as long and effectively as you have been active, news of your work, if not its impact, was bound to cross their path on occasion. The latter to somewhat comical effect, I might add."

"How do you mean? Like, I took out a certain mark, someone they had business with, and it got on their nerves?"

"More than a few times, yes. But although they were irked, they feared exposing themselves in any way to address the problem, meaning you. As we have seen, it took Ch'gal's return, and the threat of my renewed interest, to draw them out that far."

Now, Kennedy stared at him, even while Ashlee turned around as if to find the reason for the sudden quiet. "Was it you?" he said. "Were you using me against them?"

Ross said, "We were not always friends, Kennedy, so I can understand your asking. However, the answer is no. A wide-ranging operation such as the Grille was sure to run into the occasional snag whenever its own activities intertwined with earthly concerns. I of course knew when and how it was happening, that you were involved, and I admit I thoroughly enjoyed watching. But while I very well could have steered you one way or another to increase these occurrences, I thought it better to save my efforts—*our* efforts—for the single big push we are implementing now. And besides," he said, smiling again, "the randomness only made it more amusing."

Now satisfied, Kennedy said, "Well, whatever they did or didn't know, you also said they were going to figure out about us eventually."

"I said that Doge would. Of that, I am certain."

"Which makes us the only ones still in the dark." Ross was already nodding, confirming, as desired, that he knew full well where Kennedy's line of thought had gone. "Can we finally talk details here? When this is going down? What I need to do once I'm in there? How do I get to the Generator and shut it down? For that matter, how am I getting in? And what's it even like in there? I mean, shit, you made it for aliens for Christ's sake! Will I even be able to breathe?" Suddenly wondering about it, he said almost to himself, "I hadn't even thought of that."

Ashlee broke in unexpectedly, "I've been picturing it like an episode of Star Trek: The Next Generation I saw once, where this astronaut got lost in space, so these aliens made some kind of simulation for him. They based it on a book he had, I think, and all the other people were just characters, like NPCs. He was all alone."

"The book was entitled *Hotel Royale*," Ross said, "and your comparison, like your memory, is not far off." Ross didn't eat, but apparently he watched television, Kennedy thought. Or, more likely, he had plucked the information out of the ether before Ashlee had even spoken. That is, if he hadn't simply scanned the pertinent facts directly from her brain, retrieving her memories more accurately than she could ever hope to.

Ross continued, "I set it up to be very much like any similar location on Earth—a bar, with all the appropriate signage, lit by artificial moonlight. The campus itself is a blank field approximately one thousand feet in diameter, and exists in gravity identical to that of Earth. Where I had left room for expansion, believing that I might eventually add lodging and other amenities, the Council has filled the space, now using it for storage and transport of their various acquisitions. With such easy access to the many worlds, they deemed the real estate too valuable for mere accommodations. No one actually lives there.

"I should note also that although we have always spoken of it as such, it did not originate as the Grudgeville Grille. Its creation far predates any such similar establishments on Earth, but since I gave it the name, none who are familiar, including myself, refer to it any other way. It never ceased, while I was around, to serve as a kind of social waypoint for travelers, but in the beginning it resembled something more like a simple train station.

"It was meant to be an introduction, of sorts, and to always remain so. Mostly unchanging, yet always adapting, able to incorporate new technologies as humanity progressed, without any further intervention on my part. As a result, other, more advanced alien technologies find it impossible to take hold, which, in fact, is why the Generator was so difficult to develop for the likes of them, and why its name, in large part, reflects precisely how it functions, as you will soon discover. But this feature is also the reason you are able to reach them at all. Again due to their relatively minor interest in Earth, specifically, not many have adopted cellular phones, which do in fact work inside. But neither are they a stranger to the convenience they provide in speaking remotely with their contacts and agents on this side of the portal. They have even taken to the use of computers, especially in the bar. As on Earth, when currency changes hands, automation makes it easier, and does a more accurate job, of keeping track."

With the way Ross had uncharacteristically unloaded on them, Kennedy was briefly stunned into silence. Even Ashlee, who was far less familiar with how forthcoming Ross typically was *not*, seemed to understand the significance.

"How do the matchbooks fit into all that?" Kennedy said. That this question, one that never had been on his list, should be the next to come to him felt better described as more unexpected than surprising, but apparently this, too, Ashlee found notably strange, her incredulity conveyed with a look.

"They are simply a means of reaching the Grille by phone from the outside. In fact, you were mistaken, when you reached out to Doge, in thinking that by having the phone number memorized you no longer needed one. Connection is not possible without it. However, far more important is that they still work."

Kennedy frowned.

Ross said, "Just as with the safeguards I mentioned during my last visit, and in fact relating to the portals on the many worlds themselves, there are mechanisms all throughout the Grille that I created with, yet are independent of, my power. For the most part, it was simply my intent for everything to function without my constant attention, but the result is that these things are effectively immune to the Generator.

"We will not get into the ways in which that will benefit our efforts quite yet. I only tell you this so that you know: It will truly require my direct intervention to bring down the Grille, which I can only do from inside. And by its destruction, I will have atoned for yet another of my great mistakes. Or so I can hope."

All roads led back to that. And it was still surprising that Ross needed him for any part of it.

Kennedy said, "You know, you promised you'd get around to explaining that to me. And it seems to me we've got the time."

"You are wondering why I am so certain of the existence of God."

Kennedy nodded.

Ross said, "I do not subscribe to any doctrine, as you know. And never have I cared to investigate the claims of so-called prophets or their disciples. When you are certain there is a heaven it hardly matters which version it is. And certain I am."

"But why?"

"Because in my travels I discovered a place unknowable to me. In all my wisdom and experience, with all my power, try as I might, I could not enter. An impenetrable dimension, passage into which is not bought, but earned. It was a long time before I understood what it was. Only after I began to seek redemption could I truly grasp the existence of such a place."

"How do you know it isn't hell?" Kennedy said.

"Because hell will let anyone in. But I admit that when it comes to forgiveness, my hopes ride higher than my confidence. If you were to atone for your sins, heaven has a place for you. But me…"

It was strange, apparently, again, even for Ashlee, to see Ross so uncertain of anything, and suddenly Kennedy was regretting his previous comment.

Turning back to Ross, he said, "I don't know much, but I don't think it works like that. I mean, whatever you believe, if there is a heaven, I have to think it's for the faithful. All of you."

Ross was already smiling, obviously having known what Kennedy was about to say. "Thank you for that," he said. "All I must do now is everything I can. Until I have found what He wants from me."

Kennedy, if only to lighten the mood, then said, "Well, as sure as you are that no one's got it quite right, you sure do stick to convention. You always refer to God as a he."

"It is mainly for your benefit. Nearly every monotheistic religion I have encountered considers its deity to be male. I myself find it counterintuitive since I would expect that any being believed to be responsible for creation, or birth, if you will, would be viewed as female by her followers. However, I do not believe that either is actually correct. An all-powerful god, responsible for the creation of all life in the universes, would most certainly be sexless in my estimation. What reason would such a being have to choose one or the other? God has no need to procreate as other beings do. Though I admit it is a convenient way to think of such an entity. It seems that even I have gotten used to it."

Fourteen

They had been going over contingencies, Mr. Thule stating that whatever it was Mr. Doge was planning they had to accept the fact that when the time came there would be little to nothing any individual member of the Council could do to contribute to the efforts. If they weren't prepared by now, they were no more likely to be when the hitman was knocking on their door. Why he wasn't already was a question all its own, but in any case, not Mr. Thule, Messrs. Fio or Ceyon, nor anyone but perhaps Mr. Doge himself was bound to join the fight. As a result, councilmembers had been stealthily slipping through the portal without returning for over a week. Mr. Thule didn't dare depart so quickly "lest Doge take notice," he had said, but that didn't mean, as he had also said, "that we are going to risk our lives just to win points with him."

Mr. Thule had been referring to the two of them, and after being called away, Halan had found himself dreadfully alone.

"Penny for your thoughts?" He had been almost in a trance, staring at the corner of Mr. Thule's desk, when Qazaen appeared in the doorway. When he saw her, she said, "You've heard the humans say that?"

He swallowed. "I've heard *of* it, ma'am."

Coming inside, she took a seat next to the door. "And?" Then, crossing her legs, clasping one set of hands together while the other rested on the chair, palms against her thighs, she proceeded to watch him, as if waiting for some sign of life.

"Oh, I couldn't bother you with my concerns, ma'am. The Council— I'm not even— Mr. Thule wouldn't approve."

"Well, you and I are the only ones here, Halan. And as your superior, I insist."

She wasn't much older than him, he didn't think, but had a way of carrying herself that garnered a level of respect far exceeding that which he felt obligated to give most anyone else in the organization. Even the way she hadn't hesitated to sit, whether Mr. Thule was in or not, spoke to the idea that she simply belonged. He had no way of knowing whether others saw her the way he did, but wondered if this might have attributed to her having a position on the Council in the first place. All he knew for certain was that what he had just witnessed, something so simple as the way she entered a room, was something he could never have done.

"I was just…" It felt too dangerous to voice his specific doubts. "I've been thinking about… my life."

"Your life?"

"The choices I've made."

She nodded. "You have regrets." Then, "What being ever lived who had not regret?"

That sounded familiar. "What… what is that from, ma'am?"

"I don't know. But I know it is true." He retreated back into his thoughts. "Halan, how do you feel about the work we do here?"

It was like she had read his mind. Suddenly he was terrified that if he answered honestly, as a member of the Council she would be obligated to execute him on the spot or something. At the same time, he couldn't help but remember the state he had been in when she found him.

He had thought he knew what it would mean to work for the Council, the types of activities they engaged in, but he hadn't fully understood. And though only weeks ago he had begun to believe he was getting used to the kinds of vicious, bloody interventions the lately deceased Gurba and those working for him had been tasked with, he knew now that he couldn't have been more wrong.

Mr. Doge seemed to have some kind of vendetta against the hitman, but even before he was an obvious threat to them, their recent tactics during the events involving Ch'gal could only be described as unnecessarily cruel. As far as Halan was concerned, the Council had earned what was coming to them. And now he was dreading that he deserved to be counted amongst their ranks.

"It does not matter, Halan," Qazaen said now. "Consider it rhetorical. Just know that none of us is here because we got everything we wanted. Still, we must try. If there is anything you can do to fix your dissatisfaction, the time is now. And what that means to Doge, or Thule, or any of the rest of us, has nothing to do with you."

"Just leave?" Halan said. "I can't believe it's that easy."

She smiled. "Hence, you are still here."

Fifteen

They were back in the living room, having talked into the early evening, Kennedy and Ashlee sitting on one of the sleeping pads while Ross sat across from them on the floor. The other pad, along with the blanket, they had used to set up a bed for Lab in the dining room. He was still in there now, their long conversation apparently having bored him to slumber.

Ross stood, appearing as though he was planning to go, when Kennedy said, "So what about this portal? You said you would tell us how it happens to be so close." It wasn't that the question hadn't been looming somewhere in the air all day, considering the other topics they had discussed. Kennedy had just been biding his time, saving it for when they ran out of other things to talk about. And now he wasn't about to let Ross sneak away without an answer.

It had felt like the thing to do, anyway, but keeping it there at the forefront of his mind as he had, waiting for the right moment to ask, had left him more agitated than he had bargained for, and it seemed now that he couldn't avoid shooting himself in the foot. Before Ross could speak, Kennedy said, "Let me guess. Add it to the list of things you didn't want to get into today?" Honestly, Ross had answered so many other, more longstanding questions that even as Kennedy said it he thought he really couldn't complain if Ross didn't give him much in response.

"You are partly correct," Ross said. "Many of the details concerning the Grille are best reserved for another time. However, you are right to ask. It is no coincidence. For now, and because after the fun we have had today you will find it amusing, I will tell you simply that the portal was not always in its present location. And though it would seem to have put them in better proximity to you now…" For a few seconds, he looked like he might actually chuckle. "…moving it has long proven to be a pleasantly significant inconvenience for them."

Seeing his face, all three of them were soon smiling. Then, after another moment, Ashlee said, "Inconvenience how? Where was it before?"

"Most recently, only minutes outside of what is now Glasgow. I have moved it at various times through the eons, as developments on the planet provided greater interest. But the most recent change has proved the most fulfilling. They have been thoroughly annoyed by it ever since."

Ross was right, not that Kennedy, nor apparently Ashlee, had doubted it. That *was* amusing.

Neither of them thought to ask whether something interesting there was what had led to his adopting the local accent.

"So what's the real reason?" Kennedy said.

"That will have to wait until next time. But trust me when I say you will thank me for it later. I have already given you both more information than you can reasonably handle."

Kennedy could only capitulate. But although he rolled his eyes slightly as he glanced at Ashlee, he really wasn't complaining. "If I said my head didn't hurt again, I'd be lying."

Ross said, "Then with that, we will leave you. But Lab and I will be back before long."

"Let me get him," Kennedy said, reacting when Ross suddenly looked toward the dining room. "You blink him around so much as it is he's probably traumatized."

Ashlee stood as he did, and he shuffled across the room, certain it was no secret to the others that he only wanted to say goodbye. After all, Ashlee had gotten more time with him in their last couple of visits than Kennedy had in all the years since he had met him.

As he reached the corner, he realized he was trying to be quiet so as not to wake the little guy even though that was exactly what he was off to do. But as soon as Kennedy spotted him, he saw it didn't matter either way. Lab's eyes shifted to meet his, already awake, but unmoving, apparently still in that post-nap zone, familiar to humans alike, of being too comfortable to get up.

"Hey, buddy," Kennedy said. He had never called him that before, but it felt natural. "Looks like it's time to go."

Lab rose slowly now, still watching Kennedy until he was overtaken by a big yawn. He then stepped off the blanket and onto the hardwood, his nails clicking and scraping slightly as he sank into a deep stretch.

Kennedy crouched to meet him as he stood again, and Lab laid his head in his palms as Kennedy began to scratch under his cheeks. "You were a very good boy in here all day, weren't you? A very good boy." He caught himself. "I must sound like an idiot right now. I mean, with the way you and Ross communicate… You're probably beyond baby talk, at least."

Embarrassed, Kennedy let his hands drop, only to have Lab raise a paw and swipe it against his upper arm, near his shoulder. But not like he was asking for more pets. He did it twice, as if to say, *"There, there."*

Lab then watched him, and, on Kennedy's lead, began moving calmly for the living room, his nails clicking away once more until they reached the carpet at the border. He was so well behaved that if he didn't look so young it would have been easier to believe he was an old boy rather than still a puppy. Then again, he was older than he looked, so maybe it made sense.

Ashlee and Ross appeared to have been chatting when they entered, for which Kennedy was thankful because they seemed to have forgotten he was in the other room doting on the dog. They both smiled when they saw Lab, who then rejoined Ross, and after a last goodbye the two walked out the door, just as they had arrived, as though they were off to their next destination on foot.

Once they were gone, the plan became the same as any other night. The plan, at least. Ross had given him so much to think about that Kennedy wondered if he would sleep.

Sixteen

A new week had passed without a peep from Ross, and Kennedy was starting to think that if it wasn't too soon to see a pattern emerging it would be another week still. If not some unspecified number of years, god forbid, like the old days. But while he wasn't exactly pleased for this to be dragging out as it was—especially considering that even Ross couldn't be sure what the Grille might try to throw at him once he was in there—it seemed the toll was greatest on Ashlee. What had started as an agreed-upon general displeasure with being stuck here indefinitely, biding their time in whatever ways they could come up with, some more enjoyable than others, had become an exercise in not dying of boredom. And if he was only busting at the seams, then Ashlee had lost all her stuffing.

Ever since Ross's visit, she'd been different. Not emotional, he couldn't say that, but maybe moody. Even detached, in a way. Ross hadn't brought them much in the way of good news, that was true, but overall it had seemed… like a decent day, at least. Sure, Kennedy had been disappointed himself not to have gotten more into the nitty gritty of what they were dealing with, and to have learned that they were going to continue to have to wait when they had already been trapped inside for weeks. But that she should be acting more affected than he was?

The only thing he could think of was that Ross hadn't taken her side when Kennedy brought up how she was expecting, when the time came, to enter the Grille with him. Part of the prevailing tension lately might have been her simply wanting this to be over as much as he did—if not more—but if she was waiting for him to tell her he had changed his mind, that she could accompany him inside and finally finish it, her disappointment was only going to get worse.

He was glad she hadn't brought it up again. He knew eventually she would. So when they decided to order takeout that afternoon and eat on the patio, it seemed like a blessing at first the way Ashlee skipped right past it and wanted to talk about after.

"After the Grille is done?" Kennedy said.

"Yeah. Ross will shut it down, and it'll be over. What then?"

He shrugged. "Whatever we want." Ross hadn't told them exactly what he meant that night at the motel, only indicating that once the Grille was no longer a factor they would be free. He should have thought to ask why he was so sure. Maybe Ross just being Ross had giving him no reason to question it. But if being free of it all meant no more running and no more hiding, it seemed as good an answer as any.

The look on Ashlee's face told him it wasn't. "You mean you don't have a plan?"

"I don't know. I mean, I haven't really thought about it. There's a lot going on at the moment, wouldn't you say?"

"Lately, sure. But what about before? All those years? We had plans for a life together. Maybe they got shot to shit, and maybe we were dreaming considering how my father disapproved, but look at us now. We have another chance. You're telling me in the last month you haven't thought about it?"

"What's the rush? We're together. Isn't that enough?"

Again, her face was all the answer he needed. So much so that he was beginning to wonder if this wasn't what had really been bothering her. In all the years they were apart, with no hope, no reason to think it was possible, that they would ever be together again, he had missed every day the life they had envisioned together. It still wasn't on their terms, but now that it was happening? To him, it seemed a good enough start.

"What about you, specifically?" she said.

"What do you mean?"

"I mean, once it's all over, you... what? You see yourself doing this forever? Just a few weeks ago you said you could get used to this. You've been thinking about that much, at least."

"You mean my work?" Ashlee nodded. "That was just an offhanded comment. Who wouldn't want to float around in the pool all day? I mean, once you've done it enough you'd probably get sick of it, but you know what I mean."

"So you're going to keep at it."

Genuinely confused, he said, "Bad guys still need killing. You never had a problem with it before."

"That just it. *I* still don't," she said, emphasizing some meaning in it that he was apparently missing. "But you only discussed it with Ashlee. Things are different now, or have you forgotten? You could only guess before how Darling felt about it. Never—not once!—has it occurred to you to ask *me*."

Seventeen

After she stormed off, a handful of french fries, half a cheeseburger, and a ketchupy napkin were all floating or sinking in the pool. She wasn't wrong. The majority of Kennedy's life had been about what he wanted, even when he had thought he was doing it for her. "Her" being Darling. But even though Ross had helped him rectify that little problem, the very night they met, reminding him that Darling had lost more than he ever had, Ashlee had just made it perfectly obvious that he was still failing.

From the first moments after her reawakening in the parking lot of Richard's Motel, all the thoughts and feelings and memories of a past life rushing into Ashlee's mind, those of a present life into Darling's, they had begun to discuss, whenever they came up organically, the various things that one or the other regarded as new. Things like how blind Darling had been to her father's corruption, up to and including how he had put out a contract on Kennedy after Darling's murder, both of which were topics he had only discussed with Ashlee. Kennedy's poem, which Ashlee had found, its meaning explained, stopping far short of the tender moment they had shared when Darling herself had found it, something both women now knew. There was even a moment, really a whole evening, where Darling cried for Ashlee—essentially feeling sorry for herself, but rightfully so—when she stopped to consider the part of her, or them, who hadn't known her biological father and had instead faced a monstrous step-father who would rape her, at only five years old, behind the back of her neglectful, alcoholic mother.

Feelings that Ashlee had long navigated and come to terms with had overcome Darling in a way that Kennedy couldn't have anticipated.

The continued exercise had helped him to recognize quickly the wild dichotomy that would make up the personality of his beloved forever after. And yet he had failed to understand, as unexpected and blessed as it was, the full scope of the situation: that Darling was here every bit as much as Ashlee.

In the years leading up to his discovery of the elusive Ross Wellington, his own death growing ever more imminent, he had been plagued with concern over what Darling would think of the man he had become. It had been Ashlee with the impetus for him to finally come up with a good answer. And with an answer given, he had apparently put it out of his mind to the point that what Darling *actually* thought no longer mattered. At least, not enough that it occurred to him to ask.

She had also reminded him, strange as it seemed she would need to, that he hadn't always been like this. In the short time they'd had before Darling was murdered, before he ever knew Ashlee, before even her mother, Maggie, had ever been born, they had planned a life. The details were never entirely filled in. How could they be when they couldn't predict the reaction of Darling's disapproving father? But naïve though they may have been at the time, it was what she knew. And though there was no way to know just how they might have lived, what either of them would have done for employment or what prospects they, especially Kennedy, would even have had without Jacob's blessing, it was an absolute fact, considering how he had become what he was now, that if Darling had lived, their life would never have been this.

But this was what it was. And he had justified it knowing how Darling had despised predators. "People who victimize others," as he had once explained it to Ashlee. It was why she was so struck to now understand her father's true nature. Perhaps, even, why she had reacted more strongly to Ashlee's childhood torture than she might have any other person suddenly reliving a past they had thus far been blessedly unaware of. Ironic, he thought only now, that Ashlee had been one to live such a childhood. Or was it more ironic that Darling had developed such strong feelings about it when she wasn't?

Her experience had had more to do with what she saw in the newspapers during the war. What she later learned from the veterans returning from Europe in the course of her volunteer work, which her father had vehemently discouraged, and perhaps should have been a sign of the man he truly was. It was his disapproval of such activity that had led him to practically beg her for administrative help at his office, effectively removing her from her chosen work. Jacob was no Hitler, just a son of a bitch. He could have hired anyone, but she was devoted to him and he knew it. And if there wasn't enough irony to appreciate already, it was during this time that she and Kennedy found it hardest to fight their feelings for one another, and not long before they realized they no longer could, to hell with what Jacob might say. Darling's concern was always that her father would never approve of her being with someone who worked for him, as though it made them too lowly, while Kennedy was sure that if he crossed Jacob Harbor he would never find work again. Perhaps most ironic of all was how much more dramatic, and deadly, Jacob's reaction had been than anything they had imagined.

But that part of their lives was over. Now, they were two people—or "two plus," they might think of it—who had been deeply in love for as long as they could remember, yet were facing circumstances so different and so long removed from where they had started that Kennedy had forgotten what he used to want, let alone that Darling had wanted it too. He had failed to consider her in more ways than one, and only now, after Ashlee's outburst in defense of her neglected half, did he think to ask himself whether that had changed. No, he decided. When they got through this, as Ross had assured them they would, they could pick up right where they left off. Better, in fact, considering Kennedy was filthy rich, and there was no Jacob Harbor to bar their path.

But he caught himself thinking it. He wasn't stupid. Wasn't about to make the same mistake twice. Ashlee was Darling, and Darling, Ashlee, and acknowledging one while overlooking the other was exactly why he was now sitting alone soaking his feet staring at bits of bread and potato in the pool. Despite knowing that she still loved him, he owed it to Darling to let her finally articulate what before now he could only assume. But he owed Ashlee something as well. Soon, they would have the chance to live the dream they always wanted—merely being together when other forces would have them apart. She had done nothing to indicate that the plans they had made all those years ago were any less attractive to her than before, but at this point, he would have to be a fool not to ask.

Eighteen

With his primary objective taking precedent—merely ensuring they were ready—the little side project he was hiding from the Council had to be treated like an afterthought. It was far from, but still it had taken a week of sporadically searching through digital archives to find an event matching the parameters. It didn't help that he hadn't remembered the exact date or location. Less that there was no one he could ask.

Now sitting in front of his laptop, several articles splashed across the screen, he stared with only a mild sense of satisfaction, seemingly no more enlightened than when he had started. The victim had been a woman named Darling Harbor, daughter of a then local business magnate, Jacob Harbor. Ch'gal had been finicky, that much was certain, but of his particular tastes, nothing was known. And yet Doge had never known him to take an interest in such affairs, so whether the father's position in the community had anything to do with his selection was as much of a mystery as Wellington's ever disapproving in the first place.

It had happened at a park, Ch'gal apparently slicing the woman open and leaving her where she lay. Annoyingly, it seemed the papers had hastily reported only what they could learn in time for the morning edition, and he could find no indication of any sort of follow-up. Perhaps because there was never anything new to report.

Whatever the case, it was more than idle curiosity that kept him digging. Nothing he had uncovered thus far was going to make his task any easier, but although the rest of his plan was nearly set, he was still operating under the assumption that the more they learned the better. As it stood, their only course of action was what he had proposed from the beginning, after the conclusion of a certain phone call with the hitman, Wellington still on the line and holding that Doge was misguided and should stay on task. Doge had been right not to trust him, the entire charade having proven to be just another piece in the game Wellington was playing. Not that they'd had a choice.

At least they knew better now.

With the chances of his learning anything more online apparently exhausted, his next steps were as plain as Wellington's betrayal. But while obtaining physical archives was one thing, reaching the hitman discreetly was another. It was the same nagging concern he had been pushing down from the beginning of his investigation. That with everything Wellington could know, even if he learned nothing beforehand, surely as soon as the hitman was aware that something was happening, Wellington would be as well. He would prevent it.

In that case, Doge could only hope that the threat itself would be enough to spark the hitman into action. And that reaching him would be so simple.

Nineteen

It wasn't like he and Darling had never argued. That's what happens when people who care about each other fuck up. Even he and Ashlee had had their share, and they had spent far less time together. Though maybe it was all cumulative at this point.

The difference was that neither of them really had anyplace else to go. Ashlee had gone back inside, but without any furniture it wasn't like she could just lock herself in one of the bedrooms until she cooled down. That is, she *could* have, but he hadn't wanted to go in and find her still pissed off in the living room only to confirm he was right to doubt it. As a result, he was still outside, now sitting in the shade against the wall of the house, when the patio door opened again.

Ashlee emerged. When she spotted him, she stepped down onto the stone and pulled the door shut behind her. "Hey."

"Hey." She was giving him no reason to, but part of him thought he should have been the one to break the seal. "I didn't want to bug you" was all he said.

She approached slowly, lowering herself onto the patio next to him. Her sad smile looked as unsure as he felt. "You don't need to apologize. It was my fault."

"No, it wasn't. You were right." He paused, catching himself, and shook his head. Despite himself and all he had just sorted through, he was already doing it again. "I felt like I was only talking to Darling just now."

"I'm just me. All of me. That's it."

"I get it. And that's the point. I was thinking of you as just the Darling side of you, and that's as bad as what got us arguing in the first place—thinking of you as just the Ashlee side. I know you're both. I haven't forgotten it. It's just—"

"Stop. You've never treated me like you forgot. I was the one expecting too much. Like, I come back to life," she said, waving her hands in front of her, making it seem as mystical as it sort of was, "and you're supposed to remember every question you wished you could ask me when I was dead? With everything else going on? We have enough—" She froze, suddenly looking as though she had made her point, and was worried she was beating a dead horse. "We'll have all the time in the world when this is over. Until then, there's enough to worry about."

It made sense when she put it that way. Even when it came to Ross, everything he had been telling them, and everything he hadn't yet, there were so many things Kennedy had long wanted to know he was sure he had forgotten some of those, too.

Still, he couldn't help but feel like Ashlee was only letting him off the hook. "It was a big question, though. One I really haven't stopped thinking about."

"And I'll expect an answer. Eventually. For now, let's just table the future talk and focus on what needs to be done. Okay?"

It being one of those situations where there was no other way, he did the only thing he could. He agreed.

For as good as it should have been to have that resolved, even temporarily, Ashlee's expression was no less solemn than when she had sat down next to him. She was staring toward the pool, and when she caught him still looking at her she immediately stood and went to fish the remnants of her lunch out of the water, quickly realizing she would need to strip to get it all.

If this was what had been bothering her lately, why didn't it feel like they had gotten back to where they were before?

There was still the issue of her wanting to join him inside the Grille, which hadn't come up since Ross's last visit, and he was not going to bring up now because it would only get them arguing again. But she had been pissed when he told her he wouldn't allow it. Pissed, not emotional, not like she was now, so that couldn't be it.

Then what was it? What had her calling up the past and contemplating the future even while telling him that none of it mattered until they were free of all this and it was safe to do so? With everything she was saying, why did it seem like there was something she wasn't?

Twenty

Their visitors arrived in the morning again, only this time it was after he and Ashlee had eaten. It was different, too, in that Lab was a little more animated now, more than Kennedy had ever seen him, as if he remembered enjoying their last visit—despite his having fallen asleep from boredom—and was excited for a round two.

Kennedy had been right, at any rate, about a pattern emerging. Not that weekly visits were any better than the alternative if they were going to be going on indefinitely. He would have half expected Ross to comment on his being annoyed before he could even realize he was. Instead, Ross was waiting for him to speak.

"You again? They'll let anybody down this cul-de-sac." Despite their argument yesterday, the still lingering oddity of it all, and even what Kennedy was feeling now, he and Ashlee had spent the morning in a good mood. Enough so that she emerged from the kitchen smirking at what he had said, and he knew it wasn't lost on her both the long-standing existence of "dad jokes" and the idea of it being a recent trend.

He stepped aside to let their guests in, Lab's whole backside already shimmying as though he had known what to expect after the clinking of dishes on the counter the moment before. When he and Ashlee saw each other, he raced past Kennedy, barely able to keep all four paws on the floor as Ashlee bent to meet him. (Ross had informed him how rude it was to jump.)

"Hey, you two," Ashlee said, but her eyes never left the face between her handfuls of white fur.

Kennedy, on the other hand, said, "Forgive me if I'm not as enthused as he is, Ross, but after everything, the sight of you makes me expect disappointing news."

Ashlee, already on the floor with Lab, just kept petting away, while Ross, after shutting the door behind him, said simply, "The time has come, Kennedy."

Kennedy froze. Suddenly optimistic, he thought he might have to take it back.

Ross said, "I must illustrate for you the details of my plan, and what you can expect when you enter the Grille."

As though she had heard the magic words herself, Ashlee was already staring.

Kennedy said, "It's about damn time."

Ross suggested they get comfortable.

They sat on the sleeping pads, Lab tagging along with Ashlee and laying between them where Kennedy could pet him now too. Once they were situated, Ross seemed to think better of standing and got down on the floor, facing them.

"Lay it on me," Kennedy said. "What are we looking at?" Despite their pleasant morning, he was worried Ashlee would balk at that, rightfully suspecting that "we" referred only to himself and Ross.

"First, I owe you both an apology. I have not been entirely forthcoming with either of you." He paused briefly, giving them a look as though this itself was news. "As we have already discussed, it is likely that Doge's plans are known only to himself since I have been unable to glean anything from the Grille agents I have encountered. It has been disconcerting, yes. However, my lack of insight began long before that, when Doge and his Council plotted to exclude me from the Grille completely, without my notice. After all, the extensive and complex research that surrounded the development of the Generator technology, which I have only since learned of, was not something that Doge or any one individual could have kept to himself even if he wished it.

"It was not so long ago that I believed I knew exactly how this all would end, and in fact until very recently I still had not understood the significance of my inability to foresee certain things that, given the known factors, I feel as though I should, despite whatever Doge, successfully it seems, must be hiding from me. But the truth of the matter is, though I have guided you both thus far, anticipating, and even effecting by varying degrees through the decades, your eventual reunion, when it comes to the present... I cannot foresee the outcome of these events."

Kennedy glanced and found the same look on Ashlee's face, but took no comfort in knowing he wasn't the only one surprised. Although Ross couldn't seem to determine what, exactly, Kennedy would find inside the Grille, even on top of the various other details he was uncharacteristically fuzzy on, the fact that there was so much more that was unknown, even to him, and that they somehow hadn't thought to ask him for any details about what might come after all this, seemed to show just how single-minded they had been.

Or maybe it was double-minded, concentrating on not dying of boredom while also begging in solitude to get this show on the road.

"Now, while I admit that in light of the unknowns there can be no guarantees, Kennedy, I remain reasonably confident that you will be able to handle whatever they can throw at you once you are inside. I have told you all this not only because you deserve to know it, but so you will both understand that I could not begin to attribute my apparent inadequacy if not for one element I did foresee."

Ashlee was the first to say, "And what is that?"

Ross considered them a moment.

"There is a single portal that services the Grille dimension. Think of it like the kitchen doors of a restaurant. You are familiar?"

Kennedy, assuming it was rhetorical, saw Ashlee nod.

Then, rather than wonder why Ross was actually asking, as opposed to simply knowing, he said to him, "I'm surprised you are."

"I have been around. On the one side is a permanent connection to Earth. On the other is a revolving connection of sorts that adjusts according to those entering and exiting the Grille."

"Isn't that basically just two portals?"

"No. Now pay attention. Facilitating interdimensional travel throughout the universes was not my intent, so preventing its abuse was tantamount to enabling such transit at all. Not only is there a limit to the number of beings who can visit Earth at any one time, but upon leaving the Grille through the return portal, travelers are routed automatically back to the portal from which they originated. Unfortunately, I failed to encompass the movement of inorganic material from one to the next within my precautions, which is the crux of our problem, never imagining that I would be unable to prevent such a development, or even foreseeing it in the first place."

"But how is all that managed if you're not there? Wouldn't there be... traffic jams or something?"

"Or like on Star Trek," Ashlee said, "where the patterns or whatever get mixed up in the transporter?" She blushed slightly, probably embarrassed for having referenced Star Trek again. And so soon.

"I was getting to that."

Kennedy said, "Don't let us rush you."

"As with much else, it operates independently of my power, and is therefore unaffected by the Generator: an automated, background queueing system, housed in a locked room on the second floor of the main Grille building, that, along with enforcing the other two conditions, ensures that only one portal is connected at a time.

"Together, despite their now obvious flaw, these features

have played a vital role in at least slowing the expansion of the Grille's influence. However, there is yet another feature, located within that same room, that will be the key to our success." He paused, then said, "A second portal. One of which they are unaware, though its access here on Earth is very near that of the first."

"Another portal?" Kennedy said.

Ross nodded. "At the time, I did not know why, or what it meant, nor did I understand why I could not foresee the final conclusion of my actions—our actions—involving the Grille, or what it was that would prevent me from being of assistance, but even as I was absorbing the memories from Darling's brain as she lay dead at the hands of Ch'gal, I foresaw you, Kennedy James, needing a way to enter the Grille dimension undetected."

After glancing at Ashlee again, Kennedy said, "And you think this is what it was for."

"I believe we can safely assume."

"What led you to do it?" Ashlee said. "You said you know what to attribute it to."

"The only thing that would make sense of it. It is the same reason I cannot enter the dimension I believe to be heaven. I attribute it to the will of God."

"Oh, c'mon," Kennedy said, now suddenly incredulous. "The infinitely powerful Ross Wellington? If he doesn't know it, it must be unknowable?"

"I assure you, Kennedy, that even beyond the apparent inadequacies I have already discovered, my power is far from infinite. Take, for example, that I cannot create life, which is why this tiny, blue world we call Earth first caught my attention. It would be akin to bringing back the dead, or conjuring matter from nothing. These are the dominion of God. For me to attempt them… I would never survive the process." Despite himself, Kennedy couldn't help remembering then how Ashlee had wanted to ask about some furniture.

"With that said," Ross continued, "even if I am a fool for believing in the existence of some higher power in the universe, whatever form He may take, it has no effect on our current position."

Now, Kennedy blurted, "But you're not knowing what could happen sure does. Even if I can get in by this second portal, if they're still going to be waiting for me inside, I won't stay undetected for long. Having a back door isn't very comforting, even if your guesses are better than most people's facts."

"You are correct. The roof, and thus the Generator, are accessed from the exterior of the building. There is no question that once you are discovered you will be opposed at every turn. But while I still cannot provide you with any guarantees, I truly believe that if you keep moving, and delay detection until the last possible moment, there will be little they can do to resist you. The agents who managed to report in from the motel, before you dispatched of them as well, witnessed the initial attack at distance, and could hardly describe what they saw. So, other than from Gurba's previous reports of your two brief encounters with him, Doge and the Council have no way of knowing that simply increasing their defenses inside the portal still will not be enough. You should be able to proceed on your own terms, engaging when you choose. I have determined it to be the best approach, at least. Though I cannot take credit even for this."

"What do you mean?" Ashlee said.

"I mean that despite it being common sense to desire an element of stealth, when I was inspired to create the second portal, I had, as yet, no definite designs against the Grille. I did it without knowing why, even while knowing it was necessary, placing it within the existing space to hide what I had done. And since access has been restricted from the beginning, they have zero suspicion. In fact, even now, in addition to housing the queueing system, Doge and the rest believe I used it as a literal retreat, of sorts, while at the Grille, forgetting that I can travel anywhere I wish at a whim. Even the door itself was merely a façade until I envisioned you going through it, Kennedy. Now, it is physical, locked by means that he and the others cannot understand, and any attempts to break in, whatever they be, are futile. My construction is such that they have failed repeatedly even to modify the building, which is why they had to place the roof access outside, but even if they managed to take it all down, what remained would be an impenetrable box. Such was the extent of my vision, and yet, again, I did not fully understand the need for it. Who but God could have prevented me from anticipating its usefulness?"

"But if the portal is in the same room as the queueing system, won't I be seen?" Kennedy said, less concerned now whether Ashlee knew he was deliberately excluding her.

"No," Ross said. "It is an illusion. The queueing is facilitated by means that are contained and hidden within the footprint of the so-called apartment, but occurs in a space outside of the Grille dimension completely." When he made a face, Ross said, "You do not have to understand it, Kennedy. Just know that what you will emerge into is a small room—much smaller than it appears to be from the outside of the building—with a door—the portal—that leads into the interior. And that brings me to my part."

"No, wait a minute," Kennedy said, putting up a hand. "If the portal takes you inside, wouldn't that get you past the Generator? Why can't you just use it to get in yourself?"

"An insightful question, Kennedy, warranted by my failure to explain the Generator more fully. It is not merely a barrier, as you envision, but an energy field, undetectable to the naked eye. As I discovered long ago, that was a top priority. To be awash in some sort of visible wavelength, always gazing through it, inescapably and invariably being reminded of me… Doge would not have stood for it. You will have no sense of its presence despite that it pervades every vacant space within the Grille dimension, including the apartment itself." To Ashlee, he said, "Even something like your Penny Joy would simply fail to operate while the field is up, a fact they once used to test it, though they remained unconvinced until it became obvious I could no longer enter at will."

Kennedy saw her glance to the floor next to her. She had procured the weapon because of Ross, so to hear him call it hers was only fitting. More or less out of necessity, she had even been feeding it the good ammo lately. And because real copper pennies were harder to come by these days, he found himself wondering how many rolls she had left.

"Thankfully, as I said," Ross continued," the mechanisms I put in place, and the Grille as a whole, are independent of my power, and therefore unaffected by the Generator. But I have long since denied myself credit for such features. After everything, I cannot help but wonder if they were not as inspired as my creation of the second portal later was."

"You were saying something about your part."

"Yes. I intend to create a diversion at the main portal, providing the kind of excitement and attention that will benefit your infiltration, if not, with a great amount of luck, allow you to sneak to the roof unnoticed. From the beginning, the agents on watch outside were relieved like clockwork, but in the last week it has become more regimented, and in a rather odd way, all of them returning inside before any of their replacements emerge. This leaves the access unguarded for several moments, which I would take as some kind of bait if it was not so obvious. For that reason, I do not know what to make of it. However, if I time it for when they are in position, I can detain them, relieving you, in the likelihood you are discovered, of encountering their numbers inside. And, of course, those agents outside the portals elsewhere will have little to no time to interfere if you can delay your discovery, and move quickly. That is, quickly, as only you among them—*the* Kennedy James—will have the power to do."

Nodding along, Kennedy's gaze had drifted to the floor between the three of them, but he got Ross's meaning. Flashing, as he typically thought of it due to the sudden, penetrating glow that would emanate from his eyes as he then moved with such speed that the very sight of it remained secret to all but himself. Kennedy using his own power was the first step of just about any plan. Especially those that would likely have him dodging bullets or, in this case, facing enough enemy to challenge a small army.

It was too bad he could only move like that in short bursts without passing out. If he could run, then all of their planning would be virtually unnecessary.

"Okay," he said. "So, details. When do we go? What happens once I'm in? I mean, specifically? Is it a straight shot from the second floor to outside?"

Ross then described the path from the door of the so-called apartment on the second floor to the roof access outside, and it was about as simple as Kennedy had hoped.

But it wasn't *all* good news.

"I know the wait has been difficult on you both. For that reason, and not without irony, I am going to ask you to wait one week more. Use it to get your heads straight, so that when it is time to move, Kennedy, you can do so without distraction." The statement was just vague enough that Kennedy wondered exactly which parts of he and Ashlee's recent struggles Ross was referring to. And what he thought they should do to fix it.

Ross continued, "The main portal is to the west, and just south of where the three neighboring counties intersect. I told you previously that relocating it there produced a rather amusing level of frustration for the Grille. However, my true motive was merely to keep up appearances. Just as I foresaw the need for the second portal, I knew the importance of the Grille believing I had good reason to relocate, in their mind, the sole access point. They have never understood the timing of it, since the Generator was not yet a reality when I had my vision and set out after Ch'gal. After all, had I known then what they were planning—a way to keep me out completely—I would not have hesitated as I did to deal with them first. Beyond the point where you two are concerned, I can hardly explain the genesis of all this myself. To me, all the more evidence of the will of God."

Kennedy hardly had time to roll his eyes.

"The second portal is located at the eastern edge of a small canyon farther south, the features of which made it ideal for preventing the portal's accidental discovery. It would be best to move deep in the night, so I will meet you here at 2:00 a.m. and we can teleport."

Ashlee said, "Does the Grille… Do they operate on Earth time?"

"Indeed. The Grille, as I constructed it, has no natural day cycle, but over time I instituted an artificial one to allow for predictable work schedules and evening periods, so to speak, just as it is here. Due to my affinity for Earth, I even made it circadian. It has not changed, other than when I synchronized it with the new local time after moving the portal. Despite that very little of the Grille's activity actually centers around Earth, they have accepted that a twenty-four clock is decidedly convenient.

"You will arrive well after hours, Kennedy, when the typical day workers who choose to spend their nights drinking must finally surrender and retire in anticipation of work in the so-called morning. And because no one fully resides there, other than various members of the Council sleeping in their offices of late, the observed nighttime sees significantly less activity overall. Aside from the increased presence on the grounds, it is the quietest opportunity you will have.

"Please believe that if I could have fully understood the extent of my vision, how it related to just what Doge and the Council were working on, even while remaining too ignorant to prevent it, I certainly would have included a path directly from the apartment to the roof. As it stands, the access is outside because until they had chosen where to place the Generator there was truly no reason to go up there. I may have modeled the environment after any similar Earth facility, but there are no traditional utilities. No plumbing or heating and cooling considerations. Everything works by means I devised. I never thought it would be an inconvenience."

"So, what exactly is the Generator? I mean, what am I looking for? And how do I disable it?"

"There is no looking, Kennedy. As I said, it is the only thing on the roof. Away from the building, it can be seen even from the ground. As far as disabling it, because of the restrictions on technology in place within the Grille, it not only looks and, to a certain extent, functions like the Earthly device after which it is named, as I once mentioned, but its electrical configuration is similar as well. There is a switch."

Kennedy glanced at Ashlee again. "Are you serious?"

"Very simple. And once it is down, I will enter and your path will be clear. I wish to give those remaining both inside and outside the portal, including the relative few scattered about the Earth, the opportunity to return voluntarily from whence they came, but with or without their cooperation, you will be free to exit through the main portal uncontested. I will then close the portals on the many worlds before erasing the Grille from existence. No more visitors to this still-wondrous place, but no more threats either. At least, not from the likes of them."

It was a lot, and yet it seemed as straightforward as Ross had put it. Whatever he encountered inside, the path was clear.

Kennedy heaved a huge sigh. "Alright. So this is it. Feels like it's been coming so long I can't believe it's actually time."

"One more thing," Ross said, smiling as he produced something from his pocket. "You will need this."

Kennedy gazed at the item in Ross's hand, recognizing it almost instantly. "Is this..." he said, slowly reaching for it. "But I lost it in the storage."

"I retrieved it during the explosion."

Now taking the matchbook, Kennedy flipped open the cover to find the same old number handwritten there. "Wait, what do you mean 'during'?" Ross merely raised his eyebrows. "Never mind."

Ross said, "You have always wondered about the second number, and it is important now that you know. While the apartment door does not allow ingress whatsoever, calling that number prior to entering the second portal from Earth will allow one to egress for a brief period before the door then relocks. It was merely a precaution, preventing anyone who may accidentally stumble into the portal from passing through into the Grille and getting themselves into trouble, likely killed on sight. As you will soon see, trying to get back out the same way would be equally dangerous, but placing the portal where I did is precisely why it has never happened."

Kennedy remembered calling that number back in the day, and how he had gotten no answer. It was odd now to think that no one was ever going to answer it because all it did was unlock a door to another dimension.

"Alright," he said. "A week."

As if sensing an end to their visit, Lab began to stir, Ashlee's fingers pausing, buried in his coat. She had fur halfway up her arm, and as he rose she began to wipe it free, smiling as she watched him. Then, he began to whimper.

"He needs to urinate," Ross said.

Ashlee lit up, "Oh, let me take him."

"There is no need. He will be home momentarily."

"No, why don't you go ahead?" Kennedy said. Then, to Ross, "Let her have a minute alone with him before you take off."

Ross simply shrugged, smiling as the two made for the dining room and the yard full of grass surrounding the large patio.

When they were gone, Kennedy said in hushed tones, despite that Ashlee couldn't hear him, "I've been wanting to ask you... There's something going on with her." He took Ross's expression—looking almost surprised himself, for once—to mean that with everything else, it was a weird time to bring it up. "I've been trying to figure it out, but she won't talk to me."

"Kennedy," Ross said. Now, he looked sympathetic, but his tone promised disappointment. "I know that there has been tension between you and Ashlee, but it is not my place to interfere. The best I can tell you is to try to see things through her eyes. It was not so long ago you were in a similar position."

"What position is that?"

"Coping with the prospects of an uncertain future." Suspecting it was Ross's purpose, and even without knowing what was bothering Ashlee, Kennedy suddenly felt he could relate. "Take the week," Ross said, sounding like an employer granting a much-needed vacation. "I am confident that things will be resolved in that time. Trust in your love for each other. It is the one thing that will never change."

Watching Ross's face, the words *if you say so* were creeping to mind when the patio door slid open and Lab's nails began clicking on the dining room floor. The door slid closed once again.

"We miss anything?" Ashlee said a second later, looking almost chipper now.

Kennedy wondered if maybe he could fix everything by getting a dog.

Standing at the door, Ross waited for Lab to rejoin him, watched as he did, then suddenly turned to Ashlee, smiling.

"Lab says, 'Thank you.'"

"Oh. Any time. I hate to see him go. Well, both of you."

"Soon enough," Ross said. "I expect many extended visits in the near future. Our work is nearly done." He opened the door, and let Lab out first. "Until then," he said, and then they were gone.

Now, Kennedy couldn't help but wonder whether Ross had foreseen said visits, or was just being optimistic.

Twenty-One

Just as Doge had feared, he had tried multiple times with no answer, and decided he would give it a week. If it didn't work out the way he'd envisioned, they would simply strike and let the hitman find out in due course. If Doge was right in that his plan precluded Wellington's finding out at all, let alone in time to prevent it, then the hitman would discover the hard way what had happened. The next best thing to antagonize him.

That morning, he had borrowed Thule's protégé, Halan, who it turned out looked more or less human with his lower two arms hiding under a grossly oversized jacket, and sent him several hours east of the portal, to the original stomping grounds, so far as he could tell, of all the parties who had thus far entered the sphere of his investigation. It appeared even the library that had borne him the most fruit didn't have all of its past records digitized, but they did have more of this process completed than any others he could find. He took that to mean they had more records overall, so Halan was to bring back everything he could from the period in question whether he had to buy it, bribe it, or steal it from under the librarians' noses. For one who was usually so eager to please, Halan had seemed less than enthused, if not reluctant—though he didn't dare say—causing Doge to make a mental note to speak with Thule. But the second option had proved successful, and despite that the young man who had covertly gathered the materials and even loaded them into Halan's car had an expensive level of integrity, it was a level that Halan had been able to reach.

Now poring through the bins, boxes, and binders, Doge was finding virtually nothing about Kennedy James, other than information concerning his father, who had apparently been a wealthy local businessman in his own right. Of Alfonse Guiturro, who it seemed had been a figure of wildly various repute throughout his life, he had found a great deal more. This had eventually led him back to Jacob Harbor, forming a connection that by then, while not wholly predictable, was not entirely surprising, though it still did not answer the questions he had set out to.

Then Doge turned another page, and what he saw there was like taking off a blindfold.

By Ch'gal's own account, Wellington, without explanation, had spared him all those years ago, and Ch'gal, both to insulate the Grille and because he couldn't trust that it would last, immediately went back into hiding. Considering what the Council had come to believe Wellington had planned for him, the mere fact that, until recently, he was still breathing might have set them to thinking that was Wellington's true motive for letting him live. Doge was thankful that hadn't occurred to them because it wouldn't have made any more sense than his grooming the hitman for the same purpose— infiltrating the Grille—considering, again, that if Wellington had known about the Generator technology all that time ago he would have simply prevented their developing it in the first place. Now, Doge stared at the image before him, understanding exactly what Ch'gal had done, why he was now dead, and what Wellington, the hitman, and the girl had to do with it.

From the beginning, and by necessity, his research had drawn him into the past, starting with Kennedy James and Alfonse Guiturro, on to Ch'gal and his victim, Darling Harbor, and through to her conspicuous father. It revealed nothing about how they might be connected. Nor did it explain why Ch'gal's harvesting of the girl, the one Wellington had brought back, the same one whose reincarnated form accompanied Kennedy James now, had so offended the hitman. What did was the scrap of newsprint on his desk. It was a picture of Jacob Harbor from a local paper, a write-up on the business magnate after some generous donation. And in it were him, his daughter, Darling, and his two young assistants, Alfonse Guiturro and Kennedy James.

Suddenly it was all so clear.

In the mere hours before his death, Ch'gal had stated that he not only wanted to reacquire the girl, he wanted the hitman as well. It had seemed somehow significant, but at the time they couldn't fathom what it meant. They would never know the criteria by which he satisfied his obsession, but this new connection made it obvious that Wellington had lured Ch'gal back purely for the hitman's revenge. Why Wellington had waited so long to make it happen was beyond him, but that all of it, all of the trials they had faced, were in the service of some pathetic human love story... It was nothing short of infuriating.

And yet, to Doge's surprise, it mattered very little. In the end, contrary to what he had expected, having the full picture wasn't going to change a single feature of his plan. He debated whether to bother even sharing it with the Council.

He had been careful with Halan's instructions. *"Take the highway straight east, staying just above the speed limit. After a time, I will call and give you your destination."* With no way of knowing where Wellington's attention was at any given moment, it was the best he could do. Based on Halan's success, it may even have worked. If so, perhaps his other preparations had gone equally unnoticed. With any luck, when—or if—he finally reached the hitman, even if Wellington were to learn everything in the same instant, it would be too late for him to do anything about it.

Twenty-Two

Shaving in the shower was sort of wasteful, but suddenly he was open to small luxuries. He had taken Ross's words to heart, and everything had changed. Ashlee seemed happier and more hopeful. Determined, even. Ross had assured them that once this was over they would be safe, nothing left but the future.

And all Kennedy had needed to do was make it clear what he thought that was.

Yesterday, he had found her peeking through the curtains, solemnly moving from her sketchbook, to the window, then back again. It had been so quiet in the house lately, they could hear the kids even from the kitchen.

He dried his hands, tossed the towel across the dining room and onto the counter, then joined her for a look. Her pencil paused, but only for a moment.

A girl of about ten was riding a skateboard along the street leading out of the cul-de-sac. Two younger boys ran alongside her on the grass, one of them waving a precariously long stick. The peacefulness for which the neighborhood was once reputed was being lost to a generation more concerned with things like actual living. He found he didn't mind.

"If Ross is right, and we can really end this," he said, "I can see a couple of rug rats running around someday. Not that they'd be playing in the street like these delinquents, but you know." He backed out of the window to find that she already had, and the look on her face nearly brought him to tears. For all he had been trying to communicate with her in the past weeks, it was like she had needed only some reminder that he loved her. "I hope you know I would never let my work get in the way of us. I never even planned to keep going. You just surprised me was all. But all those years we were apart? Then suddenly getting you back? Even being stuck here like this is better than anything I could have hoped for. I want exactly what I always have. A life with you."

The words had come so effortlessly it was like his brain had been keeping them a secret until then.

Afterward, she had hugged him for a long time, and so tightly that he was both sure he had said the right thing, and that things had been even worse than he had understood. And before he had heeded Ross's advice, he hadn't understood much to begin with. To see it all from Ashlee's point of view? It had taken an alien who as far as he knew had never been in love to remind him that that was half of what any relationship was.

Of course, Ross being Ross, he didn't need personal experience to know, or even feel—deeply—the needs of others. It had helped them more times than Kennedy could count, and still he wasn't sure that was a good thing.

What he was sure of was that it hadn't been this good in a long, long time. Considering the difficulties posed by Jacob's disapproval, it may never have been this good. Perspective was everything, and at the moment it was hard to tell. But as he resumed pulling the razor across his cheek, water trickling down his back, it was comforting to know they were once again making plans. They just had the little problem of the Grille to deal with.

Twenty-Three

She spread the mayo on the first piece of bread, getting half of it on her thumb because her attention was on the stairs. Putting on a face had given her an appetite, but there was something else she had to do first.

It was a hell of a thing asking a man to give up his life's work, even when he had started doing it for reasons that no longer existed. But bad guys still needed killing, and she couldn't tell him he was wrong. The question then had become, how much room would be left?

She would always fit, she had been sure of that. But in the time since they had first made their plans, so much had changed. He was the same man she had always loved, in the same sense that she was the same women. There were two of her and one of him, but despite that everything had changed, nothing was different. Except the things that were. The things she was afraid to find out.

Then yesterday, without realizing it, he had seemed to read her mind the way Ross usually did. They were back on the same page, even if he didn't fully know yet why that was so important. And so for now she had to pretend it was settled. There was still work to do, and nothing else mattered if Ross was wrong and Kennedy couldn't do it on his own. It was the work they needed to focus on now.

When she heard the water come on, she put everything down and licked off her hand, knowing he was in the shower. And because he had said outright that he was going to shave in there, she knew she had time.

After making up her mind that very morning, and

remembering their conversation with Ross, she had thought of Kennedy's huge safe, all grand and white in that empty room. How it was right there, but— Then she had realized there *was* no but. They had fallen to the floor, the handle slipping from her grasp. She hadn't spun the tumbler.

As long as Kennedy hadn't been in there since...

The carpet was soft and silent on her bare feet. To notice it was déjà vu—sneaking through the kitchen with a package for her neighbor Mr. Smith while her little bunny slippers threatened to give her away by waking her mother on the couch. Mr. Smith had turned out to be an infamous contract killer with scruples named Kennedy James, and she herself turned out to be his reincarnated love, presently, at that time, in a body far too young for either of them to recognize their connection as anything but the deepest loving friendship.

How far they had come. How much they had endured to get back where they belonged.

Or as close as they could manage.

She touched the handle, pausing to hear the water still splashing down the drain, then gave it a twist. It turned freely.

The motion-activated lights came on before the door was fully open, and with them the smells of wood and carpet comprising the shelves, metal and oil comprising their contents.

She found what she needed quickly, knowing her acquisition of it was only half the battle. Kennedy would be in the shower many minutes more, but she ought to have eaten by the time he was out because that's what she had told him she was going to do.

Not that he would have any idea she had plundered his safe and then snuck out to the garage merely because she had taken only a single bite of her sandwich in all the time he was upstairs. But he would wonder. She would have to say something, and she wasn't ready to yet. Not if it wasn't the truth.

That moment would come. And when it did, it would be too late to tell her no.

Twenty-Four

Suddenly they were having sex again. Lots of it. Like in the beginning, only better. Ashlee was always moderately aggressive, and even Darling, back in the day, had been far from timid, though arguably more on the playful side. But now it was like she had discovered some new power within herself. Another level of confidence she hadn't known existed, and Ashlee, especially, had never been lacking.

What it was that had done it he couldn't have said. Just that it was equally exciting and exhausting.

It was only three more days until Ross was going to show up and whisk them off to the second portal. He didn't know if it was all the lovemaking and the fact that Ashlee seemed down for anything he wanted, but she had managed to convince him—under heavy protest, with a stern finger in her face—to let her accompany him to the location, "But only to wish me luck. You start complaining and Ross will have you back here before you can blink. You know that." She said she did, and he believed she meant it.

He had then found himself thinking that Ashlee, just like Darling, back when it was only her, had him wrapped around her finger. Right where he wanted to be.

It was already sunset when they decided to stay in for the night, prompting Ashlee to say, "I need to eat. But first, a shower. I'm starting to stick to myself."

She was smiling, so she was at least half joking. "That's an image."

"It's more your fault."

"I know."

There was no point getting dressed, so after they showered it was leftover gyros from the night before. They had ordered all their groceries earlier in the week, and thankfully Kennedy's short, though not nonexistent, refractory periods still allowed for making meals from scratch.

"I can't get over this tzatziki sauce," Ashlee said eventually.

"Well, good news. I saved the recipe, so you don't have to."

He had been hoping to avoid any more talk about the coming mission, and so far they had. But since even he still didn't know exactly what to expect when the time came, it also couldn't last.

Ashlee said, "I guess Ross wasn't kidding about not coming by again before... you know."

"You're just thinking about Lab," Kennedy teased.

"Well, sure, but Ross too. When it's over maybe he can stay with us for a while."

"Ross?"

"Well, no, now I do mean just Lab. Though, I mean, if Ross wanted to..."

"If anything, he might hang out more, but I don't think he really 'stays' anywhere. At least, not the way we think of it. Imagine being able to take a trip to, I don't know, Europe or something, but still sleep in your own bed every night. I imagine that's what it's like being him." He hurriedly set down his sandwich and grabbed a napkin. "You did just give me an idea though."

As he made for the living room, Ashlee said behind him, "What's that?"

"I just realized I should tell Knuckles about the plan. Once this is over they won't have to worry about getting any unwelcome visitors."

Despite having called him before, then staying put since, he had thrown his phone back into his satchel out of habit.

Digging it out as he was walking back, he found it just as he rounded the corner. "Here it is."

He set the bag on the counter, and powered the phone on. It hadn't even gotten to the point where he could open up his contacts when it started pinging him with notifications.

"What is it?" Ashlee said after a few seconds, making him aware the confusion had traveled to his face.

Seventeen missed calls. And not from Knuckles. Yet he recognized the number because it was the same one that he had so easily memorized he had mistakenly believed he didn't need his matchbook to call it.

Ashlee stared as he pulled that out of his satchel now too, saying nothing more when she saw what he was holding, as though knowing, like him, that for whatever reason he was being called, it could not be good.

He dialed.

Only two rings.

"Grudgeville Grille." That same fake Southern accent he was almost used to.

The number always went to the bar, but he figured that however many phones or numbers there might be, let alone the mechanisms, including the matchbooks, that made such connections even possible, there was only one person in the whole place who would have called. "I'm looking for Doge."

"Aw, you again, honey. It's so nice to hear your voice. Is Mr. Doge expecting your call?"

"I'm willing to bet."

"*Hehe.* Hold, please."

When he noticed Ashlee still watching him in silence, he quickly slipped through the dining room and out the back, leaving her in the kitchen. It was instinctive, still operating as he had been even before they had come here. Like if she wasn't around for this, it would do all the better to keep her hidden.

The stone was warm on his bare feet, but now the air had

cooled enough that it seemed justified they had decided to stay in. Not that it was affecting him at the moment, he could just tell. The fact that he was calling Kalar Doge again had him amped up. Enough that he was starting to lose patience.

After what seemed like an eternity, there came a mild *click*. "Ah, Mr. James. So good to finally hear from you."

"The feeling is not mutual."

"No, I imagine not. In fact, I was doubtful all along I would be able to reach you. After our last conversation, I would have expected you to change your number at the very least."

Suddenly Kennedy felt like an idiot. He honestly hadn't thought of it. Doge obviously didn't know it was a burner, but acquiring a fresh one should have been an equally important objective for their little trip to the gas station a couple weeks ago.

He wasn't about to admit it.

"Been laying low. Haven't had a lot of time."

"*Hmph*. Interesting choice of words. Fast to become the story of your life, if you aren't careful."

"What are you on about? What do you want?"

"I have been anxious to tell you what I have learned. That I've figured it all out. A young Kennedy James? Jacob Harbor? I would venture to guess his daughter is living a whirlwind she never quite expected." Despite that for the third time Kennedy was technically the same age now, the period Doge was referring to was the only time he had truly thought of himself as young. Ross had told them this would happen, but it didn't matter. They had tried to kill Ashlee merely because she was inconvenient to them. He would be taking them down whether they knew the truth or not.

"So you finally got your hands dirty. Now you know why it's all going to bite you in the ass."

After a brief pause, "I wouldn't be so sure, Mr. James," and now there was a smile in his voice that Kennedy could almost picture despite having no idea what Doge looked like.

"What am I missing?"

"Oh, it's nothing, really. Only that the moment you rang I dispatched a group of paramilitary operatives to visit your friend the broker. It is possible you still have time to intervene on his behalf, but they were standing by very closely, and growing steadily more impatient while I've been trying to reach you these past few days." Kennedy's heart was racing. "Hope is a dangerous thing, Mr. James. If I told you he was already dead, I daresay I would never get you to budge. Am I correct?"

Kennedy's eyes flashed and the phone exploded in his grip, too far outside his consideration to prevent it, but when he turned to enter the house, he saw Ashlee, frozen in place, now staring across the dining room at the Kennedy she believed was still on the phone. As quickly as he could, careful not break it, he whipped open the patio door, lurched inside, and whipped it closed behind him again before switching off and calling to her, "Get dressed."

She had barely enough time to be startled when he flashed again, retrieved and put on all his gear, and was back standing before her, putting out the eyes once more before she could even begin to say "What the fuck?" which she did, though still referring to when he had first suddenly appeared inside.

It was the first time he had donned his gear, let alone his mask, in nearly a month, so he knew it was more than just his tone and intensity that got her moving in the next instant.

"What happened?" she said. "Are they coming?"

He didn't know what exactly could have led them to Shields, but he wasn't about to leave Ashlee alone now. Though as she ran naked toward her pile of things next to the sleeping pads on the floor, he did consider for a moment the logistics of dressing her himself.

"It's Shields," he said.

Ashlee paused only a split second to say "Fuck."

She never wore a bra, her panties might have been inside out, and she didn't bother buttoning her shirt. She pulled up her jeans, didn't lace her Chucks, and rather than putting on her sleep holster she stuffed Penny Joy inside, wrapped the strap around the whole thing, and tucked it inside her waistband.

The last thing she did was snatch up her bag, surprising him when she started for the garage even before he did as she began digging around inside it, things dropping to the floor along the way. At last, she flung it to the side, and shoved what she had found into her front pocket.

"Ammo," she said.

Kennedy hit the remote for the overhead door and started the bike as Ashlee climbed on behind fastening a few buttons on her shirt. She then swung her legs into his lap, first one, then the other, quickly tying her shoes as he sped out into the street.

In another few seconds, the garage door was rolling shut behind them and Ashlee was gripping his waist with her forearms while strapping her sleep holster to her wrist. Hoping there would be no need to pull them out, he was certain she had grabbed the good pennies.

Twenty-Five

The first time Kennedy ever visited the office, Shields' security had watched and laughed as he pulled up on his bike, dressed as he was, and continued to mock him as he explained he had come to speak with their boss. It had been unpleasant, not least of all for them in the end, but it was also very organized. They had worked as a unit, guarding the door in formation and not budging in their belief that Kennedy didn't belong there. Every visit since had been the same, minus the sarcasm. When he and Ashlee pulled up in the alley behind the building now, what they saw, in the bright light next to the entrance and those overhead on either side of the alcove leading to it, was absolute carnage.

The bodies of Shields' men lay strewn outside the door, blood smeared on the puffy jackets they still called uniforms and spattering the haphazard tables, chairs, and concrete where they liked to sit. There were usually half a dozen, including their leader, and Kennedy's favorite, Billy. Kennedy counted as many now, but the way they lay as he rushed for the buckled steel door, he couldn't see their faces to know who was who.

The inside was almost normal. Dim picture lights illuminating the artwork on the walls. Antique furniture making it look more like a museum than an office. The only differences were the few bullet holes just inside the door, and the many more peppering the wall and desk on the other side of the room. It was when he saw the ones in the desk that he saw the feet sticking out from behind it.

As he moved inside, he heard Ashlee step up into the

doorway, and when he crouched at Shields' feet, she said, "Oh
my god, KeBe," using the nickname Darling had given him,
even at a moment like this, because now that they were one
and the same there wasn't much else she ever really called him.
"I can't believe this," she said, now standing back and to his
left, watching over his shoulder.

Shields lay in a pool of his own blood, presumably from
the bullet wounds in his chest and arms, and one that had
managed to hit his neck. In his right hand, pointing almost
straight up where his arm was pinned between his ribs and the
bottom-left drawer of the desk, was a snub-nosed .357.

Kennedy had never known him to be armed, but
apparently even in this he had kept it classic. Based on the lack
of blood anywhere else in the office, the gun had done him no
good.

From the doorway came, "Those sons of bitches!" The
figure collapsed to his knees, framed by the glow from the
alleyway behind. "I'll kill every fuckin' one of 'em!"

The anguished face was visible even in the dimmer aspect
of the room, teary eyes staring past Kennedy's knees at the
prostrate body of the man who was like a father to him.

"Who were they, Billy?" Kennedy said.

"I don't know." Billy's face changed, immediately getting
harder. He was summoning up the effort to answer the
important questions, as though knowing it was the only way
to get what he wanted. "Professionals, for sure. Eight or ten
guys, maybe, all blacked out. Suppressed weapons." He was
already breaking down again. "We never saw 'em comin'."

The desk was a mess, Shields' bobbles and less sentimental
things tipped over and strewn about, some of them fallen to
the floor. The file cabinet was open, folders and their contents
littering the floor as well.

Kennedy said, "They were sloppy, if you're still
breathing." With a general nod toward Billy's face and clothes,
"They must have thought they hit you."

As Kennedy stood, Billy looked down at his jacket, and the white shirt underneath. Then he swiped the side of one hand across his chin, showing only mild surprise when it came back with a smear of blood.

"Jamie was in front of me when they capped him. I barely got a glimpse of them before he slammed into me, hard. I hit my head. I guess—" His gaze shifted a moment. "I can't've been out a few minutes, tops."

Along with the other files casually flung about, one folder lay open and empty at the edge of the desk. Directly below it, at Kennedy's feet, were two off-sized sheets of something that didn't look like paper. Upside down, unless they were just blank.

"You gotta let me help, Mr. James," Billy said. Ashlee had found some tissues, gone over, and was wiping his chin. To her, almost bashful despite the circumstances, he said, "Thank you, ma'am."

"It would be better if they were wet."

"Little fridge by the bookcase. But you don't have to—"

She was already up and moving to where he had pointed.

Kennedy stooped to pick up the odd-looking sheets, and knew at first touch what made them so different. They were photo paper. When he flipped them over and saw the first image, he almost wished he hadn't.

In the interest of getting on Kennedy's good side, Shields had once claimed he had no real knowledge of him. Not of his identity, or even how to find him. For the sake of him and his men, Kennedy still insisted on keeping his face behind a mask, but Shields had quickly proved trustworthy to the point that Kennedy had known it wouldn't have mattered *what* the guy knew. He put Billy in that category as well.

What Kennedy saw now proved that Shields' ignorance, even if once genuine, had not endured.

The photo was an arial shot of the property where Kennedy had later built the storage, recognizable, even in its vacant state, by the highway, the dirt road running parallel to it several hundred yards away, and the simple fact that he had seen enough similar images throughout the building process that it was unmistakable.

Ashlee had wetted a fresh wad of tissues and was back with Billy, her hand now guiding his own across his face, an open water bottle on the floor between them.

Kennedy expected to flip to the next image and find the storage in all its glory, the hideout Ashlee had once referred to as his lair.

What he found instead gave him a shock so instant that for two whole seconds he could only stare.

When they had first met, Knuckles had been in hiding for over a decade due a bogus contract that Kennedy had received from Guiturro. They had more or less agreed to a truce, facilitating the meeting in the first place, and that was how Kennedy had been introduced to Shields. The latter, in order to protect their mutual acquaintance, had sworn that he didn't, and didn't want to, know how to find Knuckles any more than he did Kennedy. But now it was apparent his ignorance had waned again.

Despite that the authorities had made no connection between Kennedy James and his neighbors down the road, the Grille, and whoever Doge had doing his dirty work for him, now had zero reason to doubt it. Kennedy had never seen it from this angle, but as he took in the image, he knew the veritable junkyard with a trailer at its center just couldn't belong to anyone else.

"We gotta go. Now."

Ashlee was on her feet before he reached her and Billy, who then spun, calling to their backs, "I owe 'em, Mr. James. I owe 'em big."

Already out the door, Kennedy shouted back, "You'll get your chance, Billy. Be ready."

Twenty-Six

Ashlee had just loaded Penny Joy, a green glow spilling across both them and the bike, when they saw flames near the trailer and sporadic muzzle flashes from several figures weaving through the shadows between the piles of junk. By the cast of the tall yard light there was only one body visible on the ground, but it seemed as though Knuckles must have already dispatched a few.

As they drew closer, Kennedy spotted him. Two assaulters with suppressed rifles were rounding some stacks of tires in single file when Knuckles hoisted what looked like a long pry bar and punched it through the grip of his other fist, sending it flying like an arrow. His own mysterious power, once used to establish a rapport with Kennedy by knocking an engine block free of its mounts, netted him two bad guys, as evidenced by the way they fell.

Where the pry bar had landed was anyone's guess, but Ashlee had apparently seen Knuckles, too, because she immediately began firing at those safely distant from him.

K'pow!-CHING! K'pow!-CHING!

In Kennedy's ear, it was like someone dropping old cash registers from an airplane. Both shots had missed, and now they were nearing the driveway, changing their angle on things, but there was still time before it got too risky.

K'pow!-CHING! K'pow!-CHING!

One went down as Kennedy slowed just enough to turn in to the property. With their friends as the backdrop now, Ashlee stopped firing, and as he slid to a halt at the bottom of the gravel slope leading up to the trailer, everything went quiet, the assaulting force suddenly aware that their target had help.

"Stay with me," Kennedy rasped over his shoulder. Being unsure of how many remained, he didn't want her going off on her own. Not when having her close meant he could simply swat any threats out of the air before she even saw them coming.

They made it to the nearest cover—a stack of old appliances and miscellaneous parts that towered over their crouching heads—and were now at the end of the yard opposite from where Knuckles had been. All that lay in front of them were the enemy and the empty highway.

However many were left, Penny Joy answered with *One less!* when Ashlee spotted him before Kennedy did and got a shot off before being spotted herself.

"Good one," Kennedy said, catching her nod in the corner of his eye.

Then, when another head and torso poked out to look after his comrade, now prostrate next to a mound of refuse that included one of Knuckles' holey boats, Kennedy—

t'POW!

—dropped him on top of his friend.

Suddenly there was shouting. "No, hey. Talk to me. Ruth!" It was Knuckles' voice. Coming from the trailer.

With the door in sight, they couldn't possibly have missed him going back inside. Even more odd, due to their ringing ears, was that they could hear him at all if he had. Yet when Kennedy turned to Ashlee it wasn't confusion on her face any more than it was confusion he was feeling. "Go help him, I'll cover you," he said, the urgency in his own voice surprising even him.

He pointed her around the left side of their cover, then signaled her to move, shadowing her from two paces behind as he watched the gaps along the path to the trailer. At the bottom of the short steps, Ashlee stayed crouched as she reached up for the door handle, and in that moment one of the strike team circled into view, not aware of Kennedy close behind her.

t'POW!

The man went down in a heap, Ashlee barely glancing as she pulled open the door, raced through, and shut it behind her.

Whatever was going on, Kennedy could only hope she would be able to help. But because it meant she was now safely inside, he holstered his .44 and walked calmy between the two nearest piles.

Ashlee found Knuckles in the kitchen, just inside the door. Ruth was lying on her back on the floor, and he was next to her on his knees. Neither was speaking, but he was looking at her like he was waiting. There were no lights on. It wasn't until Ashlee got closer that she saw the blood soaking Ruth's shirt, and the trickle flowing from the side of her mouth down her neck.

"Talk to me, Ruth," he said again, though more calmly this time, giving Ashlee the sense that he was no longer worried whether she would respond, but was only encouraging her.

Slowly, Ruth's head began to stir, a hint of something otherworldly in it. It was a feeling Ashlee had experienced once before in the presence of this woman, and when she spoke, her voice had the same strange resonance that indicated it was Ruth the Soul come to respond.

"Thaddeus…" she said, and it was like there were speakers in the ceiling not visible in the darkness, a microphone under the collar of her ruffled top, hidden from view. From her angle behind them, Ashlee couldn't see the details of her face, but knew that if she could there would be no eyes looking back.

It was all but a maze of junk in the yard, and this was the first time Kennedy had really walked through it. He had just passed a body with a partly crumpled hunk of sheet metal protruding from its chest and neck, proving that Knuckles had, in fact, been busy before their arrival. He was just rounding another turn on his search for whoever remained when a muzzle flash to his left caused him to flash in return.

It was the trick he had been counting on, being triggered by the oncoming bullet rather than his knowledge of the shot, his power being infinitely more reactive than his otherwise perfectly adequate neurons. As it slowly whizzed by where his head had been, he leaned left and snatched it out of the air with his right hand, rotating his shoulder to continue the arc overhead and then sending the bullet underhand back to where it came from, piercing the shooter's throat and blowing out the back of his skull before he could even think to fire another shot.

One of the lucky ones, if Kennedy had anything to say about it.

Ashlee could see they had fired through the now broken window and surrounding wall, holes in the high cabinets and ceiling showing the angle they had taken from the ground outside when they must have seen Ruth through the glass. Knuckles was caressing her head as she struggled to catch her breath, the blood flowing more heavily from the corner of her mouth.

In Ashlee's mind, Ruth was standing at the window, maybe doing dishes, bullets ripping toward her and then through her with nothing but glass, vinyl, and wood to slow them down. And then, unbidden, she saw how it should have gone. A wall of green energy appearing out of nowhere and effortlessly preventing it all. Ruth seeing only a flash of light before the assault team outside was whisked away to somewhere harmless, their memories wiped of the knowledge of ever being there, or even of being killers, and leaving Ruth, and later Knuckles when she told him, to wonder what had happened until maybe someday when it came up and Ross had the wherewithal to admit that, yes, it had been a situation, and he had intervened.

Just outside the kitchen area and opposite the entrance, there was a huge hole in the back wall of the trailer. It looked like it had been blown out from inside, and quickly Ashlee realized this was how Knuckles must have exited the trailer to confront their attackers. How he had gotten back in, and how they had heard him. He must have caught her examining it because he said, "We had an escape route and everything. They came so fast we didn't get a chance to use it. I should have listened to Kennedy. We should've gotten out of here like he said."

"No, Thaddeus," Ruth said suddenly, as though his self-criticism had given her the energy to speak. "We were happy here. I would rather die with you like this than be chased away."

Near the highway edge of Knuckles' collection, Kennedy stumbled across the pry bar they had seen him employ on their way in, slick with blood where it had poked through not one, but two, bodies before landing a good thirty feet beyond where they lay. As he stooped to pick it up, he flashed again.

Another shooter had snuck up to close range—within a few feet, impressively—from behind a pile of junk, a fact that was deducible before even seeing him there simply by knowing in the same instant he flashed just how close the bullet already was.

Kennedy spun, taking a step to his right, and swung the long pry bar as he stood, striking the attacker in the waist. He then dropped the implement and moved away before switching off, letting the pieces land in a wet heap behind him.

Ruth was saying, "We came here together. We loved here together. It was the life *we* wanted, and if you think, after the countless many I was forced to endure, the endless consequences of decisions beyond my power, that I have not learned to live without regret, then you may just be as foolish as Ruth was so fond of accusing."

Just about the time he was starting to hope that there was at least one left, he heard a breathless voice speaking from behind a tall pile of hoses, rope, and other things that seemed all they had in common was their ability to get tangled. He couldn't make out what the guy was saying, but it was obvious he was talking over coms, too frantic to keep as quiet as he was trying to be.

At this point needing a particular reaction, Kennedy said loudly, "Looks like it's just you and me, buddy. It's not going to be easy, but it can be fast. I just have some questions first."

"I could not love but through others until I found this life, and my only regret is that we cannot live it again. That we shall not have such an opportunity as this. Or… perhaps…"

Kennedy found him pleading over his radio for someone to respond, and when the guy spotted him Kennedy lunged forward casually to intercept the barrel of the rifle he was swinging into position, stripping him of the weapon with ease before raising him to his tiptoes with a hand clamped to his throat.

He was in obvious pain, burned and bleeding from what looked like shrapnel wounds along his left side, including a slightly mangled left arm. Probably a casualty of whatever had started Knuckles' little fire.

"You must remember Ruth fondly," Ruth said, and Ashlee couldn't help but recognize how strange it would have sounded to anyone else. "Whether she liked it or not, she afforded us all that we have. All that we ever were."

"Why did Doge send you here?" Kennedy said, eliciting a

mild confusion on the otherwise panicked face.

"Who?"

Kennedy flashed, and with a swipe of his hand the guy's already twisted left arm came off at the elbow, the appendage suddenly dangling from the grip of his own right hand before he screamed and unwittingly dropped it.

By the time he was able to speak, his breath was hitching, and drool was rolling out of his mouth. "I— I don't know who sent us! We were just supposed to— hit the old man. Get— intel on your whereabouts if we could. When we saw his files, we— recognized the destroyed site up the road from— the photos we were sent."

"I have learned much from her, Thaddeus. Whatever it takes, I will—" She winced, the pain reaching her face, and subsequently Knuckles'.

"Don't you make me any promises," he said.

She managed a smile, fleeting as it was faint, and her last words were more an exhalation than she intended. "I will find you."

Even in the dark of the trailer, Ashlee could see the blood now pooled around Knuckles' knees. He sank forward, his arms encircling Ruth's head as he buried his face in her neck.

Ashlee waited for the sobs, but in the quiet she heard speaking outside. Whether Knuckles had intended to begin mourning immediately she would never know, because upon hearing the voices himself, he laid Ruth gently down, got to his feet, and was swiftly out the door.

She followed.

The guy had misunderstood. He had thought Kennedy wanted to know why they were at this location when what he was actually asking was why Doge had sent humans to do his dirty work. Though it did confirm that he had been right before. That since the authorities had gotten nothing from

Knuckles or Ruth, the Grille had had zero suspicions about them. Still didn't. That is, depending on whether anyone on the now terminated strike team had reported back.

From the corner of his eye, he saw Knuckles charging forward, followed somewhat less enthusiastically by Ashlee. "I'm almost done with this—"

By the intensity on Knuckles' face, he suddenly thought better of finishing, instead releasing the guy, who immediately collapsed, and taking a step back.

Knuckles stopped perpendicular to the man now on the ground, raised one fist overhead like he was swinging a giant hammer, then brought it down just the same.

Kennedy flashed again as he lunged to scoop up an onlooking Ashlee in his arms, taking her several feet away to where the impact of what he had sensed was coming wouldn't knock them off their feet.

When he put the light out again, the Earth shook, and flying dirt and chunks of dry vegetation sprinkled all around them. Not fully understanding Knuckles' rage, he turned to Ashlee, who said simply, "Ruth is gone," before burying her face in his chest and beginning to sob.

The bullet holes in the side of the trailer, which he only noticed now, told him the rest. The woman—the gentle soul—he had known, was gone. Just like that. The one who had helped him after all his years of searching, ultimately leading him back to Ashlee, who was formerly, and was still, Darling, when he hadn't even known that she, they, were who he was really looking for. How could it be that she, out of all of them, was the one made to suffer?

The man on the ground now lay in a crater, his legs pointing up at an angle above the edge, the rest of him half-buried in debris. Knuckles, clumps of it tumbling off him as he moved, freed his feet from under the dirt, and began to climb out.

When he was once again at ground level, he found

Kennedy watching him, and said, "Are the rest dead?"

"They better hope so." Then, "I'm sorry, man. I don't know what to say."

"This is my fault," Ashlee said suddenly. They both looked at her, but Kennedy felt far more confused than Knuckles seemed to be. "I was so fucked up, and we weren't... I asked Ross to stay out of our heads. Give us some time to figure things out. He could've..." She shook her head. "He has no idea what's happened."

Kennedy could hardly comprehend what she was saying. So slow on the uptake was he that he was barely at the edge of wondering whether he should be upset with her when Knuckles broke in, "Not a chance, sweetie. This ain't your fault any more than it is his for tracking me down all those years ago." He had thrown a nod at Kennedy. "It's like Ruth said. More or less. I'd rather live in danger with friends than in safety with enemies."

Kennedy said, "I still don't know what to say."

"Say you'll take care of this once and for all."

"That is the plan."

"Good. 'Cause we ain't leavin'."

Without another word, he grabbed the feet of the dead mercenary and flipped what was left of him into the very hole where he had lost his head, he and his comrades, if Kennedy had to guess, soon to be buried under a brand new pile of junk.

Kennedy stalked toward the bike, and Ashlee followed.

"Where are we going?"

"We're going. We're going *now*."

Twenty-Seven

They had been riding in silence since leaving Knuckles to his work, and were already through the city, only a few miles from the portal if Kennedy was picturing the location accurately. Knuckles had let Ashlee off the hook for what had happened, and while he himself, in that same moment, hadn't possessed enough presence of mind to say a word about it, he knew now that Knuckles was right. Whenever she had done it, whatever she had said, if it was in any way her fault that Ross hadn't known to intervene, Kennedy could lay it entirely upon himself for letting things get so fucked up, as she had put it, that she had felt the need to ask for some privacy while they fixed it.

When she finally broke the silence, freeing him of his own thoughts, he wanted first for her to know that.

"Kennedy…"

"He was right, you know," Kennedy said.

"What?"

"I can't tell you how many times I've wished it wasn't so easy for Ross to read my mind." He had to turn his head slightly and shout over his shoulder to rise above the wind. It felt a little odd, considering he was trying to console her. "With the way things were… No one can blame you for having the sense to ask for it."

"Thank you," Ashlee shouted back after a pause, as if taking it in. "But all things considered, I would rather we were still fighting."

Now he simply nodded, hoping the stiff brim of his hat would help her see that he, too, would have preferred that. If it meant Ruth was still alive.

"Kennedy..." she said again.

"Yeah."

"I know you're angry. I am too. But I don't know if it's the best idea to rush in like this."

It took him a second to gather her meaning. They were departing from Ross's plan. It was still three days before he was supposed to go, but, more importantly, it was nowhere near the middle of the night, his supposed best chance. To her, it must have seemed like he was throwing caution to the wind.

"I am angry," he said. "And one way or another Doge is going to pay. But that's not why I'm going."

"It's not?"

"No. Doge did all this just to goad me, the sick son of a bitch, thinking that way they'd be ready. And if he thinks it worked, then they'll already be hyper focused on the portal. The *wrong* portal. More than with any diversion. I have to believe that'll give me more of an edge."

She apparently hadn't thought of that. Then she said, "But without Ross?"

"Not without Ross. He might be out of our heads, but how much you want to bet he's been keeping an eye on the second portal?"

When he glanced over his shoulder, she seemed to be considering that, too. "Even though the Grille doesn't know about it, and it can only be accessed one way? Sounds like something he would do."

"Yeah."

"The element of surprise. Sort of. Will it be enough?"

"It's better than nothing. It was never going to be smooth sailing all the way, but the closer I can get before they're on to me, the better. I just need you to keep sending luck my way while I'm in there."

When she stayed quiet, he almost glanced again, first

scanning the road ahead for obstructions and eyes. Then she responded.

"Oh, I will be" was all she said.

Twenty-Eight

Kennedy had turned off the highway a safe distance to the east. If the main portal was located "just south of where the three neighboring counties intersect," it would have to be to the north, but not far. The second portal being "farther south" would then have to mean the opposite side of the highway.

Ashlee had agreed with his reasoning, at least.

The dry, packed earth was flat enough that the plan was just to continue south until, he hoped, Ross caught on that they were coming. The sign came in the form of his familiar green glow, like a floodlight in the middle of the desert, buried and pointed to the sky, about four miles south-southwest of where they had started.

Ross was toning it down the closer they got, but by the time they reached him and could make out his face, it seemed like a miracle that he'd had the presence of mind to do it. Despite having questions, in the soft moonlight that dominated once again, Kennedy couldn't help but wonder why the guy looked so uncharacteristically nervous.

"You're going," Ross said simply as first Ashlee, then Kennedy, dismounted the bike. If he had been butting out like Ashlee had said, he wasn't any more for the simple fact that he would have read them just to know who was coming. And in the instant he did, he would have known why.

"You're goddamn right I am," Kennedy said anyway.

He was staring Ross in the face, trying to formulate his next thoughts, when immediately Ross, despite how agitated he still looked, proved once and for all that he was back to doing it for them.

scanning the road ahead for obstructions and eyes. Then she responded.

"Oh, I will be" was all she said.

Twenty-Eight

Kennedy had turned off the highway a safe distance to the east. If the main portal was located "just south of where the three neighboring counties intersect," it would have to be to the north, but not far. The second portal being "farther south" would then have to mean the opposite side of the highway.

Ashlee had agreed with his reasoning, at least.

The dry, packed earth was flat enough that the plan was just to continue south until, he hoped, Ross caught on that they were coming. The sign came in the form of his familiar green glow, like a floodlight in the middle of the desert, buried and pointed to the sky, about four miles south-southwest of where they had started.

Ross was toning it down the closer they got, but by the time they reached him and could make out his face, it seemed like a miracle that he'd had the presence of mind to do it. Despite having questions, in the soft moonlight that dominated once again, Kennedy couldn't help but wonder why the guy looked so uncharacteristically nervous.

"You're going," Ross said simply as first Ashlee, then Kennedy, dismounted the bike. If he had been butting out like Ashlee had said, he wasn't any more for the simple fact that he would have read them just to know who was coming. And in the instant he did, he would have known why.

"You're goddamn right I am," Kennedy said anyway.

He was staring Ross in the face, trying to formulate his next thoughts, when immediately Ross, despite how agitated he still looked, proved once and for all that he was back to doing it for them.

"I know what you are wondering, Kennedy. But even if my inability to help your friends was due in some way to God's will, it is I, these many years, who have set us along this path despite being unable to guarantee a favorable outcome. The present circumstances are the result of my machinations alone. Likewise, you are mistaken, my dear," he said now to Ashlee. "Doge's use of humans, as well as keeping his plans hidden from his counterparts, surely resulted in my gleaning nothing of the attacks. However, even before agreeing to remove myself from your private affairs, my monitoring of you both was not constant because I did not deem it necessary. I was merely checking in periodically each day. Even if I had still been watching, it is almost certain that I would not have known you had left the cul-de-sac until it was far too late."

Once again, the way Ross had put a thing made Kennedy want to bite his tongue. Even if he could in some way blame the god that Ross was so hopeful to appease, the path they were on, as he had put it, was the same one where Darling, now Ashlee, had returned to him. And besides that, he doubted that even Knuckles would be any more accepting of the Grille's existence just for the sake of not having lost Ruth. The path they were on was the one where they would finally be stopped, too.

Ross and Ashlee were staring at each other. Like she wouldn't accept his letting her off the hook.

"Ross," Kennedy said. "I need you to get Billy."

Ross's gaze broke, still looking no more composed than when they had arrived. Appearing as though he wanted to say something but didn't know what, he didn't, and without a word, disappeared.

Kennedy turned to Ashlee, preparing to ask if she knew what was up with him, when barely a second later Ross returned, a dazed, if not amused, Billy at his side, along with an assortment of pistols, magazines, and even a chest rig and plate carrier that fell into a pile at Billy's feet like he had just made a wish to a genie.

"Whoa, that was intense," Billy said. "So we're doin' this?" He tore off his jacket, then stooped and began putting on his gear.

It was his lack of surprise that told Kennedy everything he needed to know. "I take it Ross filled you in?"

"Oh yeah," Billy said, his wide-eyed enthusiasm making him look like a teenager experiencing his first buzz. "I know all kinds of stuff I didn't know a few seconds ago. Aliens. Other dimensions. But it's not strange at all. More like I just forgot, and you reminded me," he said, glancing to Ross. "It feels good. Like winnin' the lottery."

"Then as long as you're ready, Billy." Kennedy said. "We're going to go in quietly, but if the shit hits the fan…"

Now Billy's face changed. "They killed all my friends, and the guy that was like a father to me. If I get even a chance at some payback, the hell with the rest."

Kennedy nodded.

Ross chimed in, "Your reasoning for going now is sound, Kennedy, but you can be assured it will not be mere humans Doge and his Council have employed to greet you once you enter."

Ashlee said, "All the more reason for me to join."

The words nearly broke Kennedy's neck. He stood dumbfounded, simultaneously staring at her and feeling like a fool for having believed this was settled.

Billy, on the other hand, who had just gotten everything situated and picked up his black, puffy jacket again, smiled, and quickly removed a gun from one of several holsters on his LBE, offering it to Ashlee.

"I got backups on backups," he said when she looked at him.

Now Kennedy pointed at her. "No. Out of the question."

Ashlee pretended he hadn't even spoken, saying to Billy,

"Thanks, I've got mine." She then moved to her saddlebag, Ross still looking somehow disheveled and making the whole thing weirder, and pulled out what Kennedy recognized as his Glock 17. She held it in her right hand as she stuffed two spare mags in her back pocket. Penny Joy was already tucked into her pants, still loaded and glowing softly through the denim, from after they had gotten back on the bike.

But it wouldn't work inside. Not until the Generator was down.

She had planned this. That was why she had convinced him to let her come along, even just to send him off, at the time they had originally planned. And it occurred to him suddenly that this was why Ross had been acting so strange since the moment they drove up. Why he kept glancing at Ashlee, and why he was apparently at a loss for words now.

Now, Ashlee looked at Billy, saw exactly what he was carrying, and said, "I will take a couple more mags, though."

Billy had already reholstered the gun he had offered her, and now pulled two seventeen round magazines from the array of pouches stacked on his front, with plenty still left for his own Glock, holstered nearby.

It was only his broadness that allowed him the room for such a loadout. If Kennedy had had time to really think about it, he might have been a little jealous.

"No!" he said again. "You're not going in there."

Ashlee barked, "You'll take him, but not me?"

"He has his own reasons."

"And I don't have mine? Fuck you! I spent sixty years on the sidelines not even knowing I was still alive, and how many more worried I would never see you again? All I ever wanted was a life with you, so I'll be damned if I let you go in there and risk that alone. It may not be the fairytale romance I once imagined, but if we die fighting by your side, then that's what it is."

Billy, who had watched the exchange, and was still

offering her the spare mags, seemed to think she was referring to him. When she saw him standing there, his arm still extended, he said, "I'd tell you to speak for yourself, ma'am, but we're basically on the same page."

Kennedy, on the other hand, assumed she was merely referring to herself, Ashlee and Darling, as "we," and so he didn't correct Billy. But it was odd the way she was now glancing nervously between them, as though she had said something terribly wrong.

As far as he was concerned, it was *all* wrong. He had already been considering the added danger of going now rather than in the middle of the night as Ross had originally prescribed, and not least of all to Billy. Yet he also knew what Shields had meant to him, and he had promised him his chance besides. But Ashlee? He had been so certain she wouldn't go simply because he had told her he wouldn't allow it that he hadn't really considered the tactical implications of having her in there with him. But when had even Darling, let alone the more headstrong Ashlee, ever let him command her in anything? Had simply loving her made him think he had the right?

Skipping the formality of acknowledging outright that he was a party to Kennedy's thoughts, Ross, in typical fashion, cut in, "You are right to be concerned, Kennedy. Frankly, by going now, the only threat posed by having patrons in the main building will be to make escaping detection somewhat more difficult. My concern, as before, is with those outside. The masses assembled at the portal, waiting and expecting you to enter on the grounds… They continue to be mistaken as to which direction you will come from, but they will see when you do. And they are formidable. I remain reasonably assured that you alone could resist them, at least long enough to reach the Generator. But the others…"

"I don't care," Ashlee said, stepping forward between them. "I'm tired of running, tired of hiding."

"You should know as well, the agents at the main portal disappeared inside some time ago. I presume now that it was once the attacks were well underway."

The rage on Ashlee's face was directed entirely at Ross now, a fact of which Kennedy was sure Ross was aware. Not wanting to ignore her as well, he put up a hand to placate her just a moment, hoping she would know his meaning despite his mask, and met her eyes before saying to Ross, "What do you mean disappeared inside?"

"They were not relieved. At first, it seemed like only a break from the usual schedule, but as I continued to observe, no replacements emerged. I found it suspicious, but not overly concerning, and planned to come see you at the cul-de-sac later. For the time being, I reached out more widely and discovered that the other agents in the field, including those searching for you, were still active, and completely unaware of anything unusual going on. Once I sensed the two of you here, and learned what had happened, it became obvious that Doge's intent was to have those few reinforcements back inside before I could prevent it, while not tipping me off by trying to recall those stationed elsewhere."

"Those few" were now the least of Kennedy's problems. However many there were, his priorities had shifted some. Other than bringing down the Generator, his only concern was keeping the woman he loved out of harm's way. And, if he could help it, Billy. And unless he was about to tell Ashlee that what she wanted didn't matter, that her desire to fight for her beliefs and her freedom was less important to him than simply preserving her life, he would have to do it from inside the Grille.

Funny, he thought. If she were willing to compromise herself just to make him happy, he wouldn't be able to look at her the same anyway.

With a sternly pointed finger dangerously close to her face, he said, "You're six inches shorter than me. Pretend it's two feet. You stay behind me at all times, and when the shooting starts I want you hiding between my legs."

Ross was staring at her now, to the point that Ashlee was smiling at Kennedy's words until she suddenly shot Ross a look that seemed to convey whatever it was he needed to hear. Without a word, he broke with her gaze, and only sighed.

Kennedy couldn't help feeling like he was missing something.

"Over here," Ross said, leading them ten yards away to the cliff directly behind where they had found him standing. A bank of low shrubs about six feet wide and set back only a foot from the edge barred their direct access, causing them to split off to get around it—Kennedy and Ashlee to one side, Ross and Billy to the other—as Ross pointed out into space, directing their attention. To what, Kennedy was the first to ponder aloud.

"Um..."

"This is it," Ross said.

Kennedy looked to the other two to confirm they were all thinking the same thing. Then, Ashlee said, "This is what?"

"The portal," Ross said matter-of-factly. With his hand flat, he then made a horizontal, circular motion toward what would have been ground level except that it was in the open air above the canyon, seeming to indicate somewhere directly ahead of their feet. "I could not leave it in plain sight where anyone could just happen through it. Not that they could ever get into the Grille itself, but imagine the attention. Eventually, even the Council would have learned of its existence."

Leaning forward only slightly, but enough to see all the way to the bottom, Billy said, "I don't see anything but rocks."

To which Ross replied, "Naturally. But this will help."

Gazing again at the seemingly imaginary spot, they all watched as Ross's attention, in that way it always did, caused a change that happened right before their eyes despite not knowing exactly how he was doing it. The air ahead of them seemed to shimmer for a split second like the heat effect off of pavement, or hot desert sand, before a sort of hole appeared, about eight feet in diameter, floating like an oil slick on water and ringed by a soft glow that was not unlike the familiar green waves of Ross's true form. Only Billy was new to all this, but it seemed Ross had caught him up on enough things that however strange it still was, he, like the others, was able to take it in stride.

That left Kennedy with only one obvious question. "How the hell are we supposed to get in there?"

"First, you will make the call to unlock the door. Then, I think it would be easiest if you jumped. One after another. Quickly." As they all turned to Ross now, Kennedy felt as comfortable with the idea as the others seemed to look. "I could just drop you all in together, but believe it or not that would be more disorienting. And you do not want to arrive dizzy on the other side."

"So just jump?" Kennedy said. "Are you sure? I mean, is it possible you don't foresee that we're just going to fall straight to the bottom of this fucking cliff?"

Ignoring the last part, which Kennedy could only take to mean it wasn't a concern, Ross said, "It is more like a dive, really. You will need to enter horizontally in order to land on your feet on the other side. Your power, Kennedy, will allow you to negate the added velocity after the short fall. You will, however…" He paused, glancing mainly at Ashlee, apparently still as uncomfortable as Kennedy admittedly was that she was even going. "You will need to assist the others to prevent anyone slamming into the door. I remind you all that this plan, from the very beginning, was intended only for Kennedy."

Ashlee made a face at that, but avoided looking at Ross. To no one in particular, she said, "Let's get this show on the road."

Billy clapped his hands, rubbing them together. "My thoughts exactly."

Kennedy took a deep breath. "Alright, then." He went back to the saddlebag and retrieved the phone he had forgotten he was going to need. Then, he returned to the others and said, "Let's get in position."

Taking the lead, he carefully shuffled into the narrow space between the bank of shrubs and the edge of the cliff. As the others worked their way in next to him, he finally realized that the shrubs themselves had performed exactly as intended, deflecting the three of them when they had first approached to either side of where the invisible portal was. Even someone with a death wish, he supposed, coming to this remote spot to commit suicide, would have little to no chance of accidentally discovering it. Or dying anyway when they tried to pop through again from the other side. After explaining the way they needed to jump in, if Ross hadn't already said it would be easy enough to exit by the main portal once the Generator was down, Kennedy might have been freaking out about what the hell kind of awkward jump they would have to make to get back out. That is, before probably realizing that Ross would have had them covered.

"Are we ready?" he said to the others.

Billy nodded, and Ashlee said, "Let's do it."

Kennedy dialed, letting it ring a couple of times before a nod from Ross told him he could simply hang it up. Kennedy then tossed the phone to him as though he had already agreed he would hold on to hit, squeezed Ashlee's hand once, gave her a smile, and jumped.

Twenty-Nine

It was more of a dive, really, just like Ross had said, and he emerged in a space no brighter than the moonlight spilling in from the other side, until he flashed, his feet touching down as softly as he could manage, and stopped himself three feet from otherwise hitting the door like a human battering ram. With the added glare from his eyes, he now surveyed the small room, knowing that in his current state he had all the time in the world to before the others would come through.

He didn't need it. The room looked like nothing more than a large, empty closet.

He switched off, and waited only two seconds. Ashlee appeared through the portal like she was aiming to belly flop on his face. He flashed again, catching her around the waist and slowing her forward momentum carefully so as not to damage her. After setting her on her feet, he switched off again, leaving them both in the same pale light as outside.

"I can't really see anything," she said.

"There's not much to see. Yet."

He repeated the process once more with Billy, this time standing in front of his more exceptional mass to slow him down, then simply making sure he was adequately stable before letting him stand on his own.

"Holy cow, Mr. James, this has been a day already."

"Just wait, Billy. Just wait."

They gathered at the door now, the moment presumably approaching when it would lock again, but Kennedy suddenly felt the need to stress a certain point. "Just to be clear, I know you want to bust some heads, Billy, and I know what Ross said, but if we can get to the roof without firing a shot…"

"I hear you, Mr. James. I'm just here to make sure these fuckers go down. Pardon my French, ma'am."

Ashlee replied, "Don't fucking worry about it."

Then, giving them each another look, Kennedy said, "You ready?"

Billy drew one of his several pistols, holding it pointed to the ceiling at his side. Ashlee was still gripping hers from before. She answered for both of them. "As we'll ever be."

The slight glint off the simple everyday human doorknob was enough for Kennedy to locate it. He gripped it now, gave it a twist, and pulled the door open slowly, hoping it wouldn't creak. It didn't.

"It looks clear," he said, checking both ways down the short hallway outside. To the left was a dead end, so they exited quickly and shut the door before moving to the right, just as Ross had instructed.

At first glance, it was like being in a dingy old hotel. Outdated wallpaper, trim, and light fixtures. Even the carpet was like something from another time, reminding him of the floors throughout the common areas of his old apartment building—the threadbare stairs, and the space around the central atrium. He wondered if that had something to do with the building being difficult to modify, as Ross had told them it was. It seemed relatively quiet as well considering they were above a bar, but then this wasn't *exactly* like a "similar location on Earth." There would probably be no live music, or even a jukebox. And with travel being nonexistent now that Doge and the Council were running things as they were, the patrons were all workers simply winding down after a long day, no energy left to be spent on things like dancing or trying to get laid. Not that he wanted to picture either of those things. Especially given the small variety of beings he was already familiar with.

The stairs at the end of the hall went straight down to the

first floor, so they tread slowly, Kennedy spacing them out in the hopes of avoiding any creaking here either. From the moment Ross had mentioned this part of the path, the combination of loose nails and old wood giving them away had become an obvious concern. Ross had assured them none of that would happen in this place, but he hadn't been here in a long time and it just seemed like the kind of thing he could be wrong about.

As they descended, the soft din they had heard from upstairs became more than just the occasional sliding stool or clinking glass and rose to that of varied conversation and people—or whatever—moving around in a large room. At the bottom was an empty corner formed by the two exterior walls. After turning to face the interior, to the left would be a long hall that traced back along the wall it shared with the stairs, wrapping all the way through the building, and eventually leading back to the bar. Straight ahead would be the large entryway with a second set of doors on the left-hand side leading directly into the bar. And on the right, straight across from that veritable wall of glass, was the building's entrance.

Unfortunately, because there were no extras to this place—no parking lot in the back, no dumpsters in some side alley because of the magical garbage system that Ross hadn't fully explained—there were no additional exits either. The way out was the front door. According to Ross, all they had to do—"all" they had to do—was sneak over there from the stairs and pop outside without being seen by anyone behind them in the bar.

Easy-peasy.

Motherfuck.

"Are you guys ready?" Kennedy had paused on the second-to-last step so as not to be spotted standing at the bottom strategizing. It didn't mean they had a lot of time. Or that he was any less nervous about Ashlee being with him.

Billy, he liked, but the guy's destiny was entirely his own.

"Ready," Ashlee said, and from Billy, "Let's do this." And he led them forward, feeling less confident than either of them sounded.

He stayed close to the right-hand wall, the idea being that at this time of night, relatively early, it was more likely for someone to be coming in rather than going out. From that angle, they would be through the door and already past the point where they would see the three intruders moving that way, hopefully with no other reason to look down the hall.

Halfway along, it occurred to Kennedy that they could be dealing with beings they wouldn't even know how to hide from. Something with eyes that could see through a goddamn wall, for all he knew, already watching them as they crept along. But there was no change to the sounds from up ahead, and Ross hadn't mentioned the possibility of such a thing besides. He may have been having trouble foreseeing certain aspects of this operation, but with everyone and everything he had encountered in his unimaginably long existence, surely he would have noted it.

A few more steps brought the slightest relief. The first few patrons that came into view, and then the next few, and the next, were either at tables facing each other and sideways to the entrance, or at the bar with their backs to the door. It looked like a highway roadhouse in there, just as Kennedy had imagined, despite that the entryway, now that he saw it, seemed more like that of a restaurant, or a bar in some hotel. But he could tell now as well that the hall was even dimmer than it was in there, and however the outside of the building might be lit, it appeared there was very little at the threshold. An attempt to establish an ambiance, even on approach. Ross might have mentioned that beneficial little tidbit, however slight it was.

"Alright," Kennedy said, still moving, "we stay low, out the door to the right, and around the corner of the building. We don't stop till we're on the roof."

Without a word, the others continued behind him, moving as briskly as their deep crouch allowed. Kennedy swung open the exterior door, watching behind to ensure they were following and that no one else had seen them, backed out and to the right, still verifying they were all clear, and in a few seconds they were all three outside, not a single glance in their direction.

Then Billy tapped him on the shoulder.

Kennedy looked up to find Billy's crotch in his face, then looked higher to find him staring wide-eyed straight ahead. Before even noticing that Ashlee was doing the same, he knew what he would see, and now stood, turning around himself.

The first thing was actually still a surprise, and something else Ross hadn't fully described—a sort of grand staircase, fifty yards away, that started wide at the bottom and angled in toward the top where it terminated in a flat portion maybe thirty feet wide and half as deep, if he could guess at all accurately from where they stood, looking up. Both sides were lined by walls, also angling in from bottom to top, that displayed what appeared to be some of the various natural vistas of Earth, making Kennedy think of an airport, and reinforcing the idea that Ross had intended this place to be a hub of intergalactic, and interdimensional, tourism.

If Ross hadn't also said there was a limit to the number of visitors who could go to through at any one time, the sheer size of it all would have led Kennedy to believe there was no such restriction, but he supposed the point of it was simply to make the trip, if not the destination, feel all the more special.

The far third of the entire structure was covered by a scaffold system that ranged out over the stairs and past the wall on that side, terminating in a freight elevator that started at ground level and must have been the means that Doge and the Council had devised for moving their plunder. Centered toward the rear of the top area was the portal, rectangular, this one, and reminiscent of a large, overhead garage door in size, with a visible distortion in the middle denoting the vertical split between one side and the other that Ross actually had told them about. And centered in the far half of that, what was obviously, at this point, the direct portal to Earth, was Ross's shining face. His face only.

Whether its size and magnification was meant to intimidate the enemy once they saw it, the look of distress at witnessing Kennedy and the others being caught would negate any chance of that. Still, although seeing him that way was a little odd, under the circumstances it wasn't at all unexpected when Kennedy thought about it. And neither were the dozens—no, hundreds—of beings in the space between who stood staring back at the three of them with malice on their faces.

If the group he and Ashlee had fought off at the motel nearly a month ago had been eclectic, he didn't know what to call this bunch. Besides recognizing at first glance at least a dozen that were of the same race as the once formidable Gurba, the mass before them contained such a variety he thought that even in the battle to come he would never get a look at all of them.

The one good thing: Other than the ones whose primary weapons appeared to be their hardened appendages—like another being he had faced all too recently—they were armed with only guns. Weapons of Earth. Another benefit, he supposed, to Ross's design making it difficult for alien technologies to function properly in here.

That is, as long as he could keep the bullets away from Ashlee and Billy.

"You two, get to the roof. Now!"

The moment he spoke they took off, and a cry arose from the masses before them.

Kennedy flashed, ignoring those nearest to him, and lunged for the ones already steering themselves toward Ashlee and Billy. Before they had fully raised their own guns, he had drawn his machete from under his coat and taken the heads of those who had gotten the farthest. Turning, he cut back along the front of the line, lopping off limbs and leaving the bodies to levitate in his wake before lunging back the other way to do the same once again.

None but him was fully aware of what was happening, the rest virtually frozen in time as he did his work.

Near the front of the group now was the first of the ones like Gurba, beings about Kennedy's own height, but massive, with green skin, and faces like that of a toad. Having learned already what it took to truly kill them, he shoved into two other beings, carefully, so as not to destroy them before they could intercept his main target. They were barely off their feet now, but soon they would strike all in their path with enough force to render not only the one dominating creature but all those in his immediate vicinity just a tangled mass of flesh and bone. After the appropriate interval, he would finish the job.

Turning back again, he could tell that aside from the ones angled toward Ashlee and Billy and their corner of the building, the rest were now converging on him, their gazes alone saying he was the primary threat even before he could visually recognize, in this supremely slow, altered time that only he occupied, the direction of their slowly increasing density.

Saving his blade for later work, he replaced it in the sheath centered on his back and employed his fists instead.

One, two, and he lifted them off their feet to soon fly into, and through, the ones behind them. A front kick to the chest of another, and he was thankful once again that he could keep the meat intact, making a projectile weapon far larger and with more mass than anything he could carry with him.

By the sheer number of beings they had found waiting for them he knew he had barely made a dent, but wanting to observe the effects of what he had already done in order to get a measure of his progress before continuing, he first lunged back to the other side, then switched off.

The flying bodies and seemingly random sprays of blood and flesh caused only those who were close enough to witness them without being destroyed themselves to cease their cry and look momentarily horrified before rejoining the charge.

Ashlee and Billy hadn't yet fired a shot, as if they were trying to delay the gunfight until they were safely on the roof. Good thinking. But as they rounded the corner of the building, the farthest beings, who Kennedy could tell now were breaking off the main assembly to go after them, were taking aim with their pistols and racing forward. He flashed again.

Pulling knives from his vest, he placed them in the air one at a time and pushed them on a trajectory for center mass of each of the first half dozen posing a threat. Despite that they appeared to be moving so slowly they should simply fall to the ground, they would strike with such velocity that the damage would we be far more devastating than from anyone else wielding any other blade.

It had been a decent wait, so now he moved back to the toad-like creature, stopping next to what was left of its torso, and raised his own booted foot before dropping it on the center of its chest. As hoped, the flesh and bone gave way, Kennedy's leg sinking into the resulting cavity up to his knee, somehow below the ground, or surface, of the Grille dimension itself, until he felt a *snap!* like the splitting of a sturdy wooden board. Just like Gurba and the others like him who had attacked in the parking lot of Richard's Motel, wherever the creature would have risen from, it would rise no more.

Kennedy straightened his one leg as he pulled the other from the depths of gore that somehow never stained his clothes or speckled his skin. Heaving a breath from behind his mask as he stood once again on both feet, it briefly occurred to him that after all these years he still didn't know if he should consider it another power of his, or simply a benefit of the other—moving so fast that nothing ever stuck.

He lunged back to the other side.

As he might have expected, reinforcements had begun to pour from several of the outbuildings, those who had been tasked with continuing their work ahead of the anticipated siege and had only now become aware that Kennedy's attack was underway. Given their timing, Kennedy had a hunch and turned toward the main building to find he was right. Bursting through the inner doors were a dozen or so patrons from the bar—somehow allowed to keep drinking, perhaps because *they* hadn't been expected to join the fight—and alongside them a couple dozen more emerging from the hallways to either side. What the latter had been doing until now seemed a small mystery, but perhaps they had done something to earn their rest inside. How generous of their superiors.

Kennedy turned back around, and stepped to the leading edge of the crowd to his left, once again shoving several beings forward with his hands and feet to collide with the streams now flowing forward to join the rest from the opposite side of the campus. They were spread out, but they weren't many, and would soon be surprised to find their numbers suddenly thinned all the more.

Ignoring for the moment the ones charging from the main building, he lunged back to the other side of the crowd when he noticed that several beings had fired over the heads of the ones in front of them. Ashlee and Billy were nearly at the foot of the stairs, Ashlee already reaching for the bottom post of the railing in order to grip on, swing around it, and begin climbing. Seeing that the few bullets already en route had been poorly aimed and were in no danger of striking either of them, Kennedy let them fly and attended to the shooters instead, his fists quickly ensuring they would never fire again. Then, to give the two more time to reach the roof, he jumped along a line at the edge of the horde, grazing ten or so in front with his leading shoulder in such a way that they would be flung into their compatriots, each with the effect of a wrecking ball against a stained glass window. They would wipe out dozens.

Back across he went.

The method was sound, so he tried it again, this time cutting two swaths along the front of the crowd directly across from the main building's exterior doors. Satisfied, he glanced back to the other side to ensure all attention was on him, indicating Ashlee and Billy were still safely on their way, then turned around to face the few dozen about to emerge from the building, and switched off.

Behind him to the left and right, beings were stopped in their tracks as the bodies ahead of them were cut down by those of their flying comrades, flesh exploding in their faces and cutting down still others who were unlucky enough to be caught by shrapnel made of bone and clothing and even the odd supersonic glob of blood or tangle of hair. In the same moment, the front doors of the Grudgeville Grille burst open and not two or three dozen, but several, raced forward, spreading out before him and soon obscuring his view of the entire front of the building. He was surrounded. Apparently, those waiting inside hadn't been there by luck. There were planned reinforcements, in case Kennedy had come through the portal, began fighting his way through the masses, and managed to make it anywhere near the building.

He glanced at the roof, unable to see Ashlee or Billy due to what appeared to be a lip that ran all the way along it, like many flat-roofed commercial buildings. Above it was the sign, and somewhere behind it, the Generator. As long as the enemy was focused on him, the other two were free to shut it down. A simple switch. Yet they hadn't.

And still there was the oversized head of Ross visible in the portal. Outside, not yet in. He looked like a child pressing his face against the aquarium glass. Repeatedly meeting Kennedy's eyes, he kept gazing past them, past Kennedy and them all, seeming more distraught now than when he, Ashlee, and Billy had spotted him there after being spotted themselves. What was he looking at? Being surrounded, there was no way to tell.

He flashed again, and with a quick leap, step, and a few good shoves sent a third of the new participants on a path that would take them in pieces back through the glass doors from which they had just emerged.

He then lunged to his left, doing the same over there while verifying that the stairs were vacant, no sign of the others, and wondered what was the holdup on the roof.

Once more to the other side before sweeping across the mass that had closed in around him. Their bodies would open a view to the other side of the campus and whatever Ross seemed to be looking at, so he switched off, waited barely a second, and in the next instant found his question answered.

Staring back at him from beside one of the small, nearby outbuildings, was Ashlee, hiding behind some kind of metal crate while Billy ran for the next structure, a series of crates stacked there as well.

What could have happened? He knew. At the base of the stairs they must have recognized they were being shot at, ran right past them, and all the way around the building.

The plan had changed. The Generator was still up, and they weren't going to be the ones to bring it down.

Neither was he, as long as they were in the open.

Thirty

When Doge had gotten word that the hitman and two others had come from *inside* the building, it hadn't taken him long to deduce that Wellington had more tricks up his sleeve than they had given him credit for. And yet, by the sight of his face, eerily enlarged and close within the frame of the portal, they apparently still weren't enough to allow his own passage. What a fool.

The others had apparently been trying to get to the roof, a thankfully failed attempt at the Generator, to be sure, and had now disappeared behind the building. One was a large man. The other, a woman. He was certain it had to be the girl. Why the hitman would ultimately bring her here when previously he had worked so hard to safeguard her was a final mystery that Doge, at long last, had not the least desire to solve. Because if he had anything to say about it, her being here would be the worst, and final, mistake of the infamous Kennedy James. And the greatest disappointment of Ross Wellington.

Still watching from the portal, the latter appeared as yet unnoticing of Doge's presence, so as the others rushed through the door to surround the hitman, in the noise and commotion Doge stole across the front of the building, escaping even his detection, and around the corner to the staircase, finding no one, as expected. The only evidence that anyone had been here were the fresh bullet marks on the stairs, several of them, dented and shining where the paint had been taken off. With his own firearm in hand, a weapon, like so many other things here, that they were simply forced to contend with, he quickly made his way to the back of the building so as to be completely out of sight of Wellington or anyone else, then carefully peered around the next corner.

Still nothing. It was obvious now that they had gone to the other side, surely hoping to provide support from a new position. With any luck, he would catch them at the opposite corner of the building, and have them in his sights before they knew he was there.

As he stalked forward, the assault resumed, briefly, shouts and cries and the sounds of clashing bodies emanating from the front of the building. By the time he reached his next position, it had ceased once again. He had been able to see nothing when he emerged from inside, the others blocking his view, but the report from the motel only weeks ago, where their second attempt at the hitman and the girl had failed, had painted a picture that told him exactly what he would find before this was over, despite that in the previous instance Wellington had apparently cleaned up the mess, leaving their contact in the police with no evidence to corroborate the story.

He had yet to witness the hitman in action himself, but his purported speed was proving out. It was for that reason that as he shuffled along Doge was forced to endure the painfully swollen flesh at the base of his horn, and work hard to quell the impulse to simply transform and confront the hitman face to face. The battle had been raging for mere moments, the term "raging" a seeming impossibility to describe so brief a period. And yet, through a series of fits and starts, which was apparently his strategy, Kennedy James had already wiped out dozens of their best with no indication of slowing down.

As uncomfortable as it was to acknowledge, the man's power was something that even Doge could never hope to contend with, regardless of the form in which he might attempt it. But, as he reached the next corner and prepared to poke his head around, he wondered: Was it enough to protect his lover?

There she was, crouched behind a crate near one of the small, temporary staging buildings, and beyond her the male, similarly hiding behind two crates that were stacked beside another. With no environmental factors to be concerned with, no rain or snow or blowing sand, Doge regretted that the only reason they had such buildings, now being used as cover by the enemy, was to conceal from clients who wished to inspect their orders prior to taking delivery the precise quantities and availabilities of the resources in question. After all, inflated prices were only possible with limited supply.

Both the girl and her companion were now firing uncontested from their sheltered positions, which Doge took to mean that the hitman was ensuring they encountered no responding resistance. And despite the latter's efforts, the concentration of forces was apparently still sufficient that the two barely needed to aim. They didn't notice him watching from the rear corner of the main building, but neither did Doge know how to get into range without being seen.

His opportunity finally came when the girl, finding plentiful targets who were difficult to miss, rapidly burned through several magazines until she was suddenly out of ammunition.

First, she signaled to the other one, who it appeared was carrying more, and after pulling something from inside his jacket, he raised up slightly, tossing it for her to catch. Neither of them saw the one who was creeping from the shadows behind the large man. Doge didn't recognize him, either, but welcomed him just the same.

The second the magazine left the human's hand, the new player struck his opposite arm with some kind of makeshift club, snapping the bones in two and causing him to drop his gun. He was already screaming in agony before the club then struck his right leg, effectively folding him in half until he lay on his back on the ground.

His first cry had caused the girl to miss her catch, and now she was too late, fumbling to pick up the magazine after her partner was already down. Fortunately for the latter, his gun had apparently landed next to him and his still good arm, and he managed to put three bullets into his attacker's chest before the club could come down yet again.

After that, neither of them moved. But the girl did.

With her gun now reloaded, she pressed forward, taking cover behind a large piece of equipment that was sitting in the open in front of the building. Clearly it hadn't been stowed prior to the assault, but never before had they allowed Wellington to completely disrupt their work, so why should they now? When she began firing once again, Doge saw his chance.

Using the shadows on this side of the building, he stuck close to the wall, quickly reaching his final position. Now he could see the girl easily, taking a few potshots from behind one of the loader's massive tires before hurriedly ducking back into cover. She had no way of noticing him unless she turned hard to her right, and even then he was still in the dark. For the moment, at least.

As he stood, preparing to finish it, she again ran dry, and he watched as she tucked the empty pistol into the back of her pants before immediately pulling something from the front. He recognized it at once. The long missing prototype. It had disappeared decades ago, to the great misfortune of the agent who had been allowed to carry it. It had helped them immensely in their development of the Generator technology, but had proven far too complicated a product to be considered anything but a novelty. After everything, the girl getting her hands on it was simply too coincidental to be misunderstood. But although Wellington may have wanted her to have it, Doge knew that presently, even as she appeared dissatisfied with its inert state, it had no power here.

With a smile in his heart, he stepped out of the shadows.

The hitman was still surrounded, but now much farther from the front of the building, presumably why the girl took cover where she did. At the same time, reinforcements were slowly coming through from the portals elsewhere, though to what benefit he simply no longer cared. Not the girl, the hitman, nor any of his own people seemed to notice him even now, despite that he was in the open. But he knew who would.

Raising his gun, he looked toward the portal, met Wellington's gaze, and sneered, supremely pleased by the helplessness he found there. All his plans, all his plotting, about to go up in literal smoke. His inexplicable pet project, an entanglement with humans by the most powerful being Doge had ever known to exist, rendered down to a simple waste of effort at the barrel of an archaic weapon. It was a face Doge had practically prayed for as long as they had been acquainted, and yet seeing it at that moment was somehow even better than he had ever anticipated. A face that said Wellington knew even he couldn't undo this.

But suddenly Wellington's eyes broke away, his attention turning elsewhere. In the next instant, splashes of new gore erupted from the center of the battle, and suddenly the image in the portal was that of a pistol, a revolver, firing into the air. Over the heads of everyone. Toward the building. The roof.

Recognizing immediately what it meant, Doge turned his focus back to the girl, and quickly took his aim.

Thirty-One

Kennedy had led the fight away from the building, hoping to keep the focus on him instead of Ashlee and Billy—out of sight, out of mind—despite that they were firing freely into the hordes of Grille agents from their covered positions. It seemed to have worked, and now that his view was blocked by some large piece of equipment to his right, he took comfort that theirs were still the only shots coming from over there. As long as no one broke from the pack to address the threat—in which case Kennedy was ready to move again—it was probably the second best place they could be.

His eyes still blazing, glinting here and there off the stainless steel of some of the weapons pointed tentatively in his direction, his aggressors apparently unwilling to fire toward their own team for fear of being fired upon in return, Kennedy once again swept across the lines both in front and behind him. When he stopped, because of the way he was facing, he found his attention suddenly drawn to the portal. On the side nearest the main building, the side farther from where he stood now, beings were pouring through. Appearing frozen in time by Kennedy's state, and apparently bottlenecked by Ross's queueing system, they were still an obvious, steady stream that led straight from the portal and all the way down the stairs to where they were joining the fight.

Kennedy's progress was slow, but equally as steady, so the sight of that alone wasn't enough to effect his mood. What did was the unexpected sight in the Earth half of the portal—Ross, moving in time with him as only he could, but with a look of terror on his face unlike anything Kennedy had seen before.

He appeared to be staring past him, toward that big yellow machine, more like, as though it was actually a bomb disguised as an assembly of hydraulics and tires and was about to go off. Kennedy looked over there, seeing nothing that justified such concern, but when he turned back, it got even weirder.

Where Ross's face had been, suddenly there was an image of Kennedy's .44 magnum firing at an elevated angle, like seeing a clip from the battle on a TV screen. Except Kennedy hadn't used his gun yet. And why would he be aiming so high besides?

Then it hit him. The roof.

Gazing up, he realized he could now see the Generator from the ground. Ross had casually mentioned that was a possibility, but they hadn't expected it to matter. The plan had been to be up there with it.

His view was partially obstructed by the slowly expanding cloud of what used to be several individual beings now melded into one, but something had triggered Ross, and to Kennedy that meant not to hesitate.

Plunging forward into the hoard would only create more of an obstruction, and possibly negate his angle on the Generator besides, so he switched off momentarily to allow the mess to clear, his eyes already probing for what he assumed would be the Generator's most vulnerable spot—the point where the power was connected. The switch.

The beings before him, as ever, were taken aback by the sudden vaporization of those ahead of them, so while they halted for a brief moment before ultimately charging forward to their deaths, as though the next wave would somehow be more effective, Kennedy found what he was looking for, drew his gun, and flashed yet again.

Taking careful aim, he fired.

Then, knowing it was over, feeling a sense of relief he hadn't quite expected, he happily undid his mask, and switched off for good.

"No!" Ross shouted, and a wave of energy exploded forth like a supersonic ripple across a pond, causing all of Kennedy's attackers to disappear in an instant and brilliant flash. It was like Kennedy had blinked and suddenly found himself in a different place, clean, bare, and vacant. The Grille remained, but the bodies, blood, and gore, and even the freight elevator—

"Join

me

Kennedy."

He had flown by in a green blur, sweeping in from the elevated portal, right past him, and descending to the ground where only seconds ago the large, seemingly out of place piece of machinery had—

Kennedy froze.

Ross was himself again, now kneeling on the ground. Above his head, mysterious blobs of white and red, and a glimmering something that Kennedy quickly realized was a bullet, all hung in the air despite that he was moving at normal speed. Ashlee lay crumpled on her side, her dark auburn hair soaked in blood.

"Hurry," Ross said desperately. "It will happen quickly."

Kennedy stayed in real time with him, even as he rushed over, and despite the sight of her wound tearing a hole in his heart, confirming the inevitable, he was already wishing desperately not to see what he knew he would.

It happened in the next moment, a glowing orb slowly rising from the center of Ashlee's chest. Unlike when he had ended Ch'gal, releasing the countless souls he had collected, hers was so bright it was nearly white, only a hint of blue, like a pale flower. It rose slowly, Kennedy's heart aching with every inch, knowing that all too quickly it would simply drift away, higher and higher, searching its way to the heavens. He turned to Ross pleadingly, desperate for him to do something, but then, a foot above her still breast, it slowed quickly, and suddenly froze. There it seemed to pulse, almost imperceptibly, as it hovered, swaying back and forth ever so slightly as though it couldn't hold itself still. Why it had stopped there was beyond Kennedy's guess.

Again, as if in answer, it happened in the next moment.

A second orb began to rise from Ashlee, this one much bluer, and smaller, and somehow fallen behind the first, appearing from within her stomach in a way that was almost as confusing as why there would be two.

Despite that he had gotten no response a moment ago, he was about to ask. But then it struck him, and suddenly he could make sense of everything he couldn't before.

"She had not told you," Ross said now. Not asking, only knowing.

Kennedy, a firmness quickly setting in his jaw, forced a reply through trembling lips. "I think she was trying to."

Ross said solemnly, "There is difficulty in all matters of the heart, Kennedy. I have seen it proven time and again, and the two of you are no exception. Here," he said, "let me show you."

The image of things that once were flooded his mind in an instant, but as though from an unseen observer. And now the thoughts and feelings he could not have known before permeated his awareness as when they did only Ashlee's.

Ross comes through the door and greets her. "I am pleased you are doing well," to which Ashlee replies, "Oh. Uh, thanks?"

A blur, then a shift, and now she is in the bathroom, confused, then concerned, wondering about the date, until suddenly she's in the living room. "It's the fifteenth." "...can we go out tomorrow?"

He's pumping gas and she's moving away from him, for "Snacks," she says, but then, suddenly inside, she is more concerned with the contents of the small box she's torn open, her hand stuffing the item deep into her pocket.

Another shift, and now she's staring into her hands, the answer to her question eliciting a "Shit!" that Kennedy had mistaken for something else before silently admonishing herself, moments later snapping the pregnancy test in half and flushing twice to get it down the toilet.

Next they're in the kitchen, and he thinks she's still on the laptop while he prepares dinner. This time he can hear her thoughts as though she had meant him to. "God, what is he going to say? Does he even want a family anymore?" *In her own mind, the baby is developed far beyond where it presently is, though she knows it.* "We can't tell him yet. There's a job to do, and we need to focus." *It hits her suddenly, though the phrase "delicate state" had already popped into her head more than once.* "Shit. Will you be safe if I go with him?"

Another shift, and Ross is back, saying, "Not on my end," *which gives her a shock. To Kennedy's revelation now, as it was to hers, Ross had anticipated this since the motel. That was the very night it happened, Ashlee puts together, which would explain why she had missed her period when she was always—always—so regular.* "He's known all along. That's why he's been making us wait." *But Kennedy says,* "Ahh, I get it." *And seconds later,* "She's worried you're going to take my side when..."

His words fade, another slight shift, until Ashlee's voice cuts in, "Ross..." "Do not worry," *he replies, though his attention appears still to be on Kennedy, who is making his case, reiterating the details of he and Ashlee's disagreement. Their conversation travels through the air in secret, giving the words a disembodied quality, like the narrator in a commercial.* "It is not my place to tell him. But I encourage you to do so. After all, his concerns are not unfounded even now."

Soon after, he and Lab are leaving. Kennedy has gone to the dining room, and they are able to speak freely. "Ross." "As promised, I will not tell him." "That's not all I'm worried about." "I know. Give him only love and time. Soon, he will come around and remember that was all he needed." *The sound of Lab's paws suddenly clicking on the floor makes a lump in her throat, and she hurriedly wipes her eyes.* "In the meantime... I don't... I mean, how can I—" "There is no need to fear,

Ashlee. No need to feel guilty. You are thinking, 'After everything he has done—is doing—for us, how can I tell him to butt out?' You have every right. My devotion to you and Kennedy is second only to that which you have for each other, and everything I have done is merely to repair the effects of what I failed to do so long ago. You owe me nothing. I will continue to monitor the Grille's activities insofar as I can, and update you both whenever it seems fitting. But I will otherwise leave you in peace, out of your thoughts, and your affairs, until it is time to move. Knowing the two of you are safe here," he says, the scene already beginning to shift, *"it is very little to ask."*

Now they are by the pool, Ashlee staring at him while he chews. "How can he not want things to be different? How can this be enough?" *She storms off, launching the rest of her own meal into the water, but quickly there's another shift, and she's saying, as though his carelessness hadn't destroyed her, "...you're supposed to remember every question you wished you could ask me when I was dead? With everything else going on? We have enough—"* until she catches herself, because in that moment, even though Kennedy would have no way of catching on, what had come to her mind was the baby. "I'm so sorry, little one. Maybe soon." *"We'll have all the time in the world when this is over"* is what she says.

The images shift again to when things are made worse, Ross claiming that Kennedy should be able to succeed if only because the Grille has no way of knowing what he is truly capable of. "Reasonably confident?" *she thinks.* "That's supposed to make it better?"

Next, she is at the window, sketching the children down the street for reasons he doesn't yet know. He finally pulls his head out of his ass and tells her what he has always felt, that he still does, and never didn't, want a life with her, which is exactly what she's been longing to hear. A wave washes over her body like stepping into the warm sun, and she rises and hugs him tightly. "I knew it. I knew it."

The carpet in the other room is soft on her feet, and suddenly she remembers being a little girl, sneaking across the kitchen on a mission to visit Mr. Smith. She is relieved to find the safe is still unlocked, and soon she has a pistol in her hand. "Daddy isn't going to do this alone.

Not if we have anything to say about it."

Kennedy wants her to send luck his way while he's inside. "Oh, I will be," she says, and then, thinking of his borrowed gun in her saddlebag, "nine millimeters at a time."

Even Ross doesn't get the chance to protest, knowing her intentions full well from the moment they found him waiting at the second portal. "Don't say it, Ross. I don't care if you think he can handle it." *Then she lashes out when Kennedy still doesn't want her to go. "Fuck you! I spent sixty years on the sidelines not even knowing I was still alive, and how many more worried I would never see you again?" A sudden skip. "…if we die fighting by your side, then that's what it is." "I'd tell you to speak for yourself, ma'am," Billy says, "but we're basically on the same page." Ashlee heaves an internal sigh, though she may still be caught.* "Yeah, I meant you, Billy. I meant Billy."

Moments later, Ross is staring at her, "I fear for you, Ashlee Carter. I could make you stay," *until she gives him a look so intense it makes Kennedy feel like he's missing something,* "You wouldn't dare."

At long last, she is standing at the edge of the cliff after Kennedy has already jumped through, her words now, though still in her head, like the last moments of a dream slipping away. "Here we go. Time to help Daddy work."

With a sudden fade, the images departed as quickly as they had come, and now Kennedy watched as the soul of his beloved, truly the other half of his own, was joined by that of their unborn child, the former suddenly justified in its waiting. Whether the stress of the situation, the trauma of Ashlee's head wound, or even the way she fell, it had killed their child in virtually the same instant, and now they floated in the air before him, soon to be off, together in death as they were in life. Together and alone.

They hung there, almost motionless but not, until Kennedy began to suspect there was something more going on. Was it Ross? Holding them there in the same way that the bullet and Ashlee's blood, bone, and brain were still hanging mysteriously above their heads?

"No, Kennedy," Ross said. "They linger because of you."

Through gritted teeth now, Kennedy knew his unspoken questions had been as clear to Ross as anything he could do or say, and still he wished to have been wondering something else if only to have garnered a response that felt less like a dagger in his heart.

He expected these new thoughts to warrant another reaction when Ross suddenly said the unthinkable. "You wish to leave."

Kennedy turned to him in anguish. How could he say such a thing? Even knowing that his loved ones couldn't stay there forever, why would Ross want to hurry them off?

But he was no longer looking at the two souls before them. He was looking toward the building. There, in the open, several feet from the doors, was a being that would have looked almost human, in his dark suit and glasses, if not for the extra set of arms sitting just below the first. He was pressing his lips together, his gaze averted, and with both sets of hands clasped tightly at waist level it was obvious he was trying to prevent himself shaking.

"Yes," the being managed.

"You should have listened to your mother."

Nearly in tears now, from what Kennedy could tell, he nodded quickly. "Yes."

"Then remember this," Ross said. "Innocence is more valuable than all the riches of the many worlds. You never belonged here, Halan. And it is not too late to be forgiven."

With that, a tear rolled down Halan's cheek, and again he nodded.

"Go."

At Ross's dismissal, Kennedy watched Halan ascend the stairs and leave through the portal, back to wherever he had come from. Seeing him disappear felt like the herald of an ending too many, but Kennedy turned back to the glowing orbs knowing nothing he could do would delay their inevitable departure.

"I can't believe I didn't see it," he said absently. "Everything she's been going through lately... It was all my fault."

"Lovers have struggled more greatly while contending with far less, Kennedy. And communication requires two. She might have told you if not for the fear that it would unduly weigh upon you at such an inopportune time. And you had no way to know the cause of her uncertainty, even while you did well to address it.

"Unfortunately, in the same moment you had adequately reassured her, she became determined once again to help you. She is a warrior who would rather die fighting to protect her family than sit aside and let the father of her child fight alone. And once she knew that you would be everything they needed you to be, and that they would be there at your side, sharing the burden of your task, rather than tell you, she simply wanted to wait. To surprise you."

Kennedy, now in tears, could only stare as the souls of his... his family... hung in the air before him, soon to depart, never to return. To lose his beloved yet again, and now their child along with her... It felt like watching the last moments of his own life.

"If anyone is to blame, Kennedy, it is me. From the beginning, I have guided you both along the path that has brought us here despite the plethora of unknowns. I failed to recognize Ashlee's true, fierce nature. I failed even to foresee what would befall your friends, and, in truth, believed it would not. There were signs from the very start, and yet I proceeded undeterred, convinced that I could manage the eventualities even while knowing that something so simple as moving the portal, the first step along this journey, was never my will alone. I know you do not like when I speak of Him, Kennedy, but I can no longer be certain that my ability to foresee *anything* was not a gift from God."

A gift from God? Kennedy thought. For as hard-won as their lives had been, from the moment Darling had lost her life, Kennedy James had become Kennedy James, and right up until the present moment, the only one who had done a thing for them, gifted them anything at all, was kneeling right beside him.

Then, it hit him.

Desperately, he thought, maybe it could be like before. Why couldn't it? They could do it all over again. Him aging, Ashlee being reborn, and them finding their way back to one another. Only this time Ross wouldn't leave it to chance. Instead, he would put them together, knowing they had already earned it. He could even put the soul of their child back where it belonged once Ashlee became pregnant again, and they would be free to finally live the life they had worked so hard for. Why shouldn't it be like that?

"Because it is not enough," Ross said.

Kennedy turned to his friend, reminded yet again that in his presence one could never merely dream a thing. "What do you mean?"

"You deserve, both of you, far more." He was staring beyond what lay before them. Past Ashlee's body. Past her soul, and that of their unborn child. How often his thoughts and feelings would manifest themselves into recognizable human behavior, despite that his corporeal appearance was merely a visage he presented to the world.

"I think I know what He wants from me," Ross said, and his energy began to flow once more.

Waves of green, almost like tendrils, washed over Kennedy, then past him, and then out each side of the portal while another moved in the opposite direction. Kennedy finally noticed Billy, on the receiving end, lying on the ground, visibly broken until suddenly he wasn't.

"It will take all of me to fix this…"

His attention had returned to Ashlee and the two souls hovering in the air above her, his energy appearing to draw back into himself before extending forward to encompass them.

"Had Ch'gal not taken her soul that day, I could have done this then."

As Kennedy watched, the souls of his beloved and his unborn child, still slowly rising and now directly in front of their faces, suddenly froze, and then more rapidly began to fall back toward Ashlee's body with the shrinking cocoon of Ross's energy.

"It seems so long ago now, even for me. My meaningless vow... It would have been better to end Ch'gal before it even began, but I was too selfish to see it then."

Just as the orbs sank back into her body, there came a glint of light from high above. The tissues which had flown from Ashlee's head, the brain, and blood, and bone, were returning from where they had dispersed, and even the bullet, which had flown to a point above and behind where they now sat, was being recalled.

"I hope He can forgive me. For all I have done."

Finally Kennedy saw that Ross's form was changing. His legs, folded beneath him on the ground like Kennedy's own, had disappeared, and instead of the soft green rippling and shimmering of his true form he appeared to be floating on an expanding cloud of ash, wisping away as it consumed him to disappear into the upper elevations of this realm he had created, even as the rest of him continued to work.

"Perhaps I do not deserve it..."

The bullet descended between the two of them, passing in reverse through Ashlee's suddenly intact skull.

"I must give— all I have to give—"

It emerged on the other side where it then disappeared, Ross now only a head and shoulders and arms.

"Until— there is—"

The cocoon disappeared within Ashlee, no longer acting on the outside, as though she was now enveloping it instead of the other way around.

"…nothing left—"

She was already stirring when Kennedy turned to his friend.

"…and I am—"

Before the last of him rose into the heights above like gray smoke on a gentle breeze, meeting Kennedy's eyes before his final breath was stolen, Ross Wellington had a smile on his face, and it was obvious what he had been trying to say.

He wasn't gone. He was done.

It was all he ever wanted.

Ashlee's hand suddenly brushed Kennedy's knee, and he found her trying to sit up.

"Are you alright?" he said, taking her arm. "Do you… know where you are?" She was holding the side of her head, but didn't appear to be in pain. A blessing, where only a moment ago there had been a massive exit wound.

"I remember… everything," she said. Now she faced him, almost tearful. "Ross showed me everything."

Kennedy couldn't help himself. "Oh, is that all?"

Ashlee smiled slightly, shaking her head as she searched his face. "I wanted to tell you."

"No," Kennedy said in return. "I didn't make it easy." He cupped her face in his hands. "But that's over. As sure as anything I've ever done… The three of us? I can't wait."

Ashlee's smile grew, even as the tears now rolled from the corners of her eyes, soaking Kennedy's fingertips. Ignoring them, she gripped his coat and practically yanked him in for a kiss.

She caught him by such surprise that he never closed his own eyes, and so he saw it when she opened hers and immediately appeared to stare into the sky—or what would have been the sky—above them.

Through whatever barrier to this dimension Ross had created, stars were slowly becoming visible. At the sound of footsteps they found Billy approaching, and Kennedy could see behind him, to the far perimeter, that they were visible there too. All around them, with every passing second, they resolved, clearer and more numerous until, he imagined, they would find themselves simply vented into space, like being blown from an airlock in some sci-fi movie. Was it another of Ross's fail-safes, or something he had just set in motion?

Whatever it was, it was something to contemplate later.

"We gotta go."

Billy caught up having already recognized the urgency himself by the look on his face, and they ran for the stairs, Kennedy and Ashlee hand in hand.

Halfway up, Kennedy imagined them emerging on the other side with too little momentum, or the wrong angle, to land them safely back on the edge of the cliff, but then he remembered they were leaving through the main portal now, not the other, and realized he had no idea what they were coming into.

He drew his gun, prepared to flash and go to work the instant he found out.

"You don't need it," Ashlee said. "They're gone. They're all gone. Ross wiped them off the face of the Earth."

It seemed Ross really had shown her everything.

When they burst through on the other side, Kennedy found himself somewhat disoriented, but it wasn't enough to slow any of them down. There was another elevator straight ahead, and stairs, which they opted for, to the right. Unsure what might happen to their surrounding environment once the Grille itself finally collapsed, they kept moving. It was a small relief, at least, that they were in fact alone.

"Glad to see you're alright, Billy. Did Ross clue you in, too?"

Panting from the effort of climbing more stairs, Billy

glanced at Ashlee, and said, "He did. But I kinda wish I didn't remember my leg gettin' snapped in half."

When they reached the top, the space felt something like an aircraft hangar, a large rectangular door standing open to the night air beyond. But instead of exiting, now they stopped, stepping to the railing and taking a last look behind.

Across the facility and at the bottom of the veritable pit before them, the portal stood shimmering like the surface of a child's pool stood vertically on its edge, this one apparently never hidden like the one they had used to get in. Or perhaps it had been.

However else it had changed, it seemed to be growing ever more opaque, the wall behind it becoming increasingly more visible even as they watched.

"It won't be much longer," Ashlee said, and though he agreed, Kennedy could only assume she was guessing.

"Let's not be here when it disappears."

Now at a brisk but not quite so desperate pace, they made for the hangar-style door and passed through into the moonlight. There were no lights on the front of the building—at least, none that were on now—but aided by the glow extending from the building's bright interior, Kennedy's bike was plainly visible fifty yards ahead of them. Apparently, Ross hadn't wanted them to hoof it back through the desert to where they'd left it parked. There was even what appeared to be a massive sidecar attached for Billy.

"He thought of everything," Kennedy said simply.

When they started to move again, Billy said, "By the way, congratulations, ma'am. I mean, both of you."

Ashlee smiled. "Thank you, Billy."

He said, "I don't know why Mr. Wellington showed me *that*, but he showed me what happened, and that he was doing it to you too. I feel like maybe he wanted me to know what this was all about. He didn't show me everything, but I think I get it."

"What didn't he show you?" Kennedy said, wondering what Billy thought he was still missing, even while it finally occurred to him, in that same moment, that for the first time he wasn't speaking to Billy from behind his mask.

"Like, you two. I don't really know your story. Not that I need to. But he showed me lots of other stuff."

They reached the bike, and Ashlee immediately climbed on the back. Kennedy said, "Like what?"

Now, Billy smiled. "Like he showed me what happened that day you came to meet Mr. Shields. It made some sense of what happened tonight. The little I saw, anyway."

Kennedy cast his mind back to the day, disarming and beating down Shields' host of security personnel when they refused to let him see their boss. In the way that only he could. A way that Billy had never understood, and had respectfully never pried about.

"It's about time, I suppose."

Despite its size, after getting his feet in, it was slightly comical the way Billy still had to squeeze into the sidecar. Kennedy then climbed on himself.

Just as he was about to start the bike, the lights inside the building began to flicker. From deep within came a crackle, like the sparks generated by a short circuit, though it didn't seem to coincide with whatever was affecting the electricity. Within a few seconds, metal clanged where it seemed to fall from the walls, stairs, and even ceiling inside, until, finally, the lights went out and stayed out, the entire exterior began to buckle inward as though being crushed from above by a giant hand, and then everything collapsed, falling into the hole that was left and sending a giant waft of desert dust in every direction, including toward their vantage point.

"That was something," Ashlee said.

Kennedy pushed the button on his little remote, then put the bike in gear. "Let's get out of here before we can taste it."

Thirty-Two

Domestic life was a concept Kennedy had abandoned a literal lifetime ago, and Ashlee's only examples were a father that had successfully hidden his true, illicit nature from both her and her mother, and a second set of parents who weren't fit to take care of themselves, let alone a child. But within weeks they fell into it like they had been doing it all along. Oh, what they wouldn't have given.

They were spending even more time in bed than usual, things so tenuous previously that they couldn't begin to feel guilty about it. And apparently their lovemaking had been so good from the start it hadn't even occurred to Kennedy that he hadn't flashed during sex since their very first time, the night at the motel. It was that night that he had thought of one day exploring with Ashlee what might be possible. When he finally put the question to her, she agreed like it was her idea.

Furniture came, until the living room perfectly matched the picture Ashlee had drawn, now framed on the wall. Lab—still Lab, because neither of them had the heart to rename him—had a bed next to the stairs. They had found him waiting there for them after dropping Billy off. It seemed Ross really had thought of everything. But then who would forget about their dog?

By then, the rest of the cul-de-sac was fully aware of their new neighbors, too, what with the occasional barking, and all the big deliveries. For the most part, they left them alone. It helped that Kennedy's policy was to almost never answer the door. But the patio now had seats, and the bedrooms had beds. And theirs wasn't the only house getting the attention. Kennedy had fully furnished both of the other properties as well.

One was to rent. Maybe. The other, and he had already told him as much, was for Knuckles. After Ruth was killed, Kennedy had guessed wrong. Instead of burying the ones who had murdered her and covering the ground with a new pile of junk, Knuckles had buried them, then went on a cleaning spree, getting rid of every last scrap of unusable shit that Ruth—the Human—had always wanted him to. What was left was some spare parts and the tools and equipment necessary to continue engaging in the work he enjoyed most—fixing up old cars. As well as space to build a small shop, and a place, to honor Ruth the Soul, where he could lay the former's body to rest.

He couldn't see fixing the trailer, or even going on living there without her for much longer, so Kennedy had made the offer. He seemed to be warming up to it.

Ashlee was at the kitchen table, one leg folded beneath her, when Kennedy came downstairs. He was wearing only the lounge pants he knew she liked, and as he began pouring a cup of coffee, he caught her staring at him. "What?" he said, fully expecting her to comment, yet again, on the visible gap between his abs and his hip bones.

Ashlee, knowing exactly what he was thinking, hoped not to jar him too much with her question, but felt she had every right not to put it gently, either. "Are we ever going to get married?"

The moment she said it, Kennedy was reminded, yet again, not to take anything for granted when it came to her.

He smiled, placing the pot back on the burner. Without picking up his freshly-poured cup, he turned, and slowly approached.

"Well, for once we have nothing else on the docket," he said. "And I think it's been a long enough engagement. It also turns out that I found the two best women in the world, and I get to have them both."

Now he made salacious eyebrows at her before kneeling and taking her hands in his.

"Ashlee slash Darling, you have brightened every corner of my existence, and made a man out of me in every way possible. I won't ask for much. Just one more lifetime. Give me only that, and I will—" His throat hitched at the words. "I will give you all I have to give, until there is nothing left. Be my wife. Finally."

Ashlee leaned forward and took his face in her hands, his hopeful face that seemed to look at her as if there were some possibility of her denying him. She kissed his eyelids, one, then the other, as they closed, anticipating her approaching lips. She slid her arms around him, brushing her face against first his ear, then his neck, before placing a gentle kiss there. Then she clasped the back of his head, and felt him smile against her as she whispered into his ear.

"Let's go."

18 Months Later...

Rosemary Welma James.

Were they wrong to do it? They couldn't very well honor Ross without honoring that mild cornball side he somehow possessed as well.

Rosie lay in her crib, staring at the shiny medallion her parents had hung over the horizontal rail. One of the baubles that used to decorate Shields' desk, it now dangled from a rope secured through the hole at its center, shifting whenever she moved and shimmering in the soft glow of her nightlight. Lab had wandered in, as he often did, and now he lay on the rug in front of her dresser, sleeping. He wasn't growing any faster now that Ross was gone, but his coat was undoubtedly showing tinges of yellow, as any so-called white Lab, even one of his supernaturally reduced age, eventually would.

As he snored gently, his head facing the wall, Rosie noted that the door was slightly ajar, the width of a dog's body. Then she pulled herself up, taking the medallion in the palm of her hand to examine the polished copper. And like her namesake before her, the longer she looked, the more she understood, until, at last, she ran her thumb right through it, letting it pass through the material as if her contemplation of the thing involved mixing her essence with the atoms of that element.

Acknowledgments

This has been one of the longest journeys of my life. At this point, I've spent almost as much time with Kennedy James and company as I did raising my kids. They came to me in the winter of 2006-07, and now I've put the finishing touches on the final manuscript of the trilogy in the summer of 2023. Sixteen-and-a-half years. I never imagined it taking so long.

Along the way I lost my friend Danny who also happened to be one of my first and most encouraging fans, and by the time this book is published I'll have met my first grandchild. I hope never to spend so much time on any single project again—literary, that is—but not for the reason you might think.

I've enjoyed every moment I spent with Kennedy, Ashlee (and Darling, the two of whom I often referred to in my notes as Ashlee/Darling), Ross, and all the rest, including the times I almost didn't. But the simple fact is that I took much too long to finish their story, and they just didn't deserve it. For being so patient, I have to thank them first. Not only for forgiving me (spoiler, they do) but for letting me tell their story. They say picking your favorite story is like picking your favorite child, neither of which I would ever attempt or even presume to think I could, but no matter what I produce in the future or how I or anyone else feels about it, this series has a permanent, unchangeable place in my heart.

Next, it's only natural to thank everyone else who waited so patiently. Believe me when I say that if I didn't plan to be working on this so long, I certainly didn't foresee keeping anyone else waiting. And unlike Ross, I can't attribute it to the will of God. I can't even claim that I didn't always have this planned as a trilogy, and if the open ending of the first book didn't give it away there's also this, which some of you already know: The first thing I wrote after finishing book one was the last chapter of book three. More specifically, the epilogue. I knew how the series would end about twelve years before I wrote the book.

In my defense, I didn't really know how the rest of book three was going to go yet, and though I had book two firmly in mind from the very beginning it wasn't yet written, so there's that.

I wish I could say my major lack of productivity was due more to just being tired and busy raising children, but that wasn't it either. At times it was just laziness. At others, I didn't believe in myself enough to continue. For looking past all that, taking this extra-long ride, and sticking it through to the end, I thank you, and it is you to whom this book is dedicated. All I can hope now is that you find it was worth it.

Lastly, and always, because they're the most important and deserve to be most recent in my mind, I have to thank my family. Your love and support through this and all my projects is a bright spot even on good writing days, and a lifesaver on bad ones. Especially my wife, Jenni. I would likely go insane while sitting next to you on the couch and whispering to myself as I tried to figure my way out of a plot hole if I didn't have you to remind me to shut up and watch the movie.

And if that isn't a metaphor for all of life, I don't know what is.

Also by Joseph Hess

I Chose Vengeance
Bullet & Blade
Rendezvous Moon & Things Far Less Erotic
Luna City

For updates and more, go to josephhess.com, and follow "thejosephhess" on Instagram, Twitter, and Facebook.

About the Author

Joseph Hess is the author of several novels and many other stories to date, with more of each always on the horizon. When he isn't working, reading, or dreaming of seeing his characters on the big screen, he likes watching golf videos, even though he doesn't make time to play, and video games, which he's inclined to play too much. He's also a staunch supporter of the serial comma, in deference to his friends, pizza and beer, and enjoys Brazilian Jiu-Jitsu, lifting weights, and sometimes forcing himself to run. He and his wife live in Florida with half their children.

Made in the USA
Columbia, SC
15 November 2023

26093337R00112